The Girl with the Dragon Heart

Also by Stephanie Burgis

The Dragon with a Chocolate Heart

The Girl with the Dragon Heart

STEPHANIE BURGIS

BLOOMSBURY
CHILDREN'S BOOKS
LONDON OXFORD NEW YORK NEW DELHI SYDNEY

BLOOMSBURY CHILDREN'S BOOKS
Bloomsbury Publishing Plc
50 Bedford Square, London WC1B 3DP, UK

BLOOMSBURY, BLOOMSBURY CHILDREN'S BOOKS and the
Diana logo are trademarks of Bloomsbury Publishing Plc

First published in Great Britain in 2018 by Bloomsbury Publishing Plc

A catalogue record for this book is available from the British Library

ISBN: PB: 978-1-4088-8077-7; eBook: 978-1-4088-8076-0

2 4 6 8 10 9 7 5 3 1

Typeset by RefineCatch Limited, Bungay, Suffolk
Printed and bound in Great Britain by CPI Group (UK) Ltd, Croydon CR0 4YY

To find out more about our authors and books visit www.bloomsbury.com
and sign up for our newsletters

For Ollie Samphire.
I love you even more than stories!

CHAPTER 1

Once upon a time in a beautiful, dirty, exciting city full of people and chocolate and possibilities, there was a girl so fearless and so daring that ...

No, wait. I've always been good at telling stories. But this time, I want to tell the truth.

The truth is that, for once, my older brother was right: it *wasn't* sensible for me to accept the crown princess's challenge. A thirteen-year-old girl from the riverbank, with no proper home or schooling, setting out to mix with royals, match wits with vengeful fairies and stand up for her entire city? Anyone in Drachenburg could have told me that was absurd.

But there's one other truth I know for sure: if you have the courage to tell your own story, you can remake the world.

'Behold!' I pushed open the swinging doors to the kitchen of Drachenburg's finest chocolate house and strode inside, waving a freshly printed promotional handbill – one of hundreds that would be circulating through the city by nightfall. 'My latest masterpiece! Feel free to bow down to me in wonder and amazement and shower me with all your gold.'

Standing at the closest counter and stirring something that smelt delicious, the head chocolatier rolled her eyes at me. 'Oh, good,' Marina said. 'You've written more nonsense about us. As if we didn't have enough customers to deal with already!'

The doors behind me swung open as she spoke, and Horst, the maître d', hurried in, his lean brown face alight with interest. 'Show me, Silke.'

With a jaunty bow, I handed over my work, then stuck my hands in the pockets of my bright, twice-mended scarlet jacket and rocked back and forth on my booted heels as I waited.

I'd switched to wearing boys' clothing years ago for eminently sensible reasons. Wearing trousers instead of a constricting skirt, I could run as fast as the wind through even the busiest city streets. With a plain, dark green jacket and trousers, a white cravat and a green hat that hid my short black curls, I could fade into any crowd I chose. Today, though, I wasn't looking for camouflage or for escape. Today, I was ready to strut like a peacock and enjoy my well-earned rewards.

The kitchen really did smell amazing.

I reached towards the closest bowl, but Marina smacked my hand away, her fingers warm gold against my dark brown skin.

'Not that one! It isn't ready yet. Look.' She pointed to the next counter, where eight delicious-looking chocolate creams – my favourite – were cooling in long-stemmed glass bowls. 'Eat one of those', she told me, 'before you pop from sheer self-satisfaction.' She scowled. 'And then show me what you've written about us this time.'

I *knew* she'd want to read my handbill! 'Here.' Humming, I pulled out a second copy from the pocket of my only-barely-stained silver waistcoat, one of my best finds from my brother's market stall on the riverbank. 'I brought an extra one for you and Aventurine.' Then I frowned, looking around the bright white kitchen as roasting cocoa beans rattled in the hearth with a companionable clatter. 'Where *is* Aventurine?'

The Chocolate Heart's apprentice chocolatier was the most ferocious girl I'd ever met, and the most fabulous one, too ... and not just because of her unusual powers. Aventurine was the whole reason I'd found my post here at the Chocolate Heart: actual *respectable* work in a real shop with walls, serving some of the most powerful people in the city. It was the first chance I'd ever had to show my skills to the world, and I was determined to make it my first step towards a big and glorious story of my own ... one that did *not* include sleeping in a tent on the riverbank forever.

But what was the point of showing off my latest triumph if my best friend wasn't here to see it?

'I sent her to the traders' market,' Marina said, plucking the second handbill from my grip. 'We need more sugar. The loaf they gave me this morning was hollow, so Aventurine's going to tell them it was rubbish and get them to replace it for free.'

'You sent *Aventurine* to do that?' I stared at her. 'By herself?'

Marina heaved her big shoulders in a shrug as she looked down at the new handbill. 'She's my apprentice, isn't she? She has to learn. She might not pick the very best on her first try, but –'

'I'm not talking about the quality of the sugar,' I said impatiently. 'What if they're rude to her when she tries to return the first lot, and she loses her temper?'

Marina looked up from my handbill to give me a deeply satisfied smile. 'Then they'll learn not to fob us off with substandard sugar, won't they?'

'Argh!' I squeezed my eyes shut in anguish.

Did *no one* in this chocolate house understand the concept of good publicity?

It was hard enough to promote a chocolate shop whose chocolatier refused to come out of her kitchen to charm her patrons – Marina would never learn to be polite to important people – but between Aventurine's stubbornness and my storytelling skills, we'd finally managed to overcome that hurdle. Aventurine had won the patronage of the king, and I'd told the whole story to the world through a series of brilliant handbills scattered across the city to lure in new customers every day. But even I couldn't think of any way to twist our story into a happy ending if the Chocolate Heart's apprentice got so angry that she accidentally spat flame in public.

That was the problem with having a best friend who had been born a dragon before a wandering food mage had turned her into a human and left her with food magic of her own. Her transformation had worked out well for all of us, since her massive, scaly family had negotiated an alliance with our powerful crown princess – the first known human-dragon alliance in all of history – and Aventurine had found herself a new home at the Chocolate Heart. Still, even as I'd written handbill after handbill about that victory, I'd had a niggling fear growing at the back of my mind.

Now that Aventurine had figured out how to use her new-found powers to shift back into her dragon body whenever she wanted to, I was just waiting for the moment she lost control of that shift – because whoever first created the phrase 'fiery temper' had definitely had dragons in mind.

If she did lose control, I had to be there – and not only for Aventurine's sake.

'I've got to go.' I spun around to leave, abandoning my poor, lovely, untouched chocolate cream.

Before I could push open the doors to the front room, Horst looked up from his copy of the handbill and grabbed the sleeve of my scarlet jacket. 'Silke, wait.'

5

Finally! I skidded to a halt despite the oncoming crisis, raising my eyebrows expectantly. 'Yes?' I'd been waiting all day to see his reaction to the new handbill. I couldn't wait to find out which line was his favourite!

But instead of expressing his admiration for my brilliance, Horst frowned, looking past me towards the clock. 'Don't forget to be back by one', he said. 'We have a lot of bookings this afternoon, and we'll need an extra waitress to handle the crowd.'

'I *know*.' I had to stifle a dragon-like growl of my own. Didn't *anyone* understand me, even here? I wasn't reckless – or a child, no matter how young I looked.

I might only be thirteen years old, but I'd grown up on the night I'd lost my parents six years ago, on that terrible journey that had led me and my brother Dieter to our patchwork home on the riverbank of this city ... and no matter how hard Dieter had fought to control me, I'd been looking after myself ever since then. I knew perfectly well how to keep track of time!

Rolling my eyes, I pulled free of Horst's grip and slipped through the kitchen doors, clamping down hard on my frustration. 'But first I have to save that trader!' I called back before the doors closed behind me.

Then I flashed a bright, happy grin at the customers who'd turned to watch me from their tables in the bright golden-and-orange front room of the chocolate house. 'Don't forget to tell all of your friends', I told them as I hurried past, 'you ate the best chocolate in Drachenburg today!'

I kept my saleswoman's smile all the way through the chocolate house and out of the front door ... until I stepped out of view of the Chocolate Heart's big front window.

Then I *ran*.

CHAPTER 2

The Chocolate Heart was planted smack in the middle of the wealthy merchants' district, with bright pink and blue buildings and expensive carriages everywhere. It should have been a lovely sight on a brisk autumn day like today, but I didn't have time to appreciate the spectacle. The traders' market where Marina bought all of her supplies was a full two miles away, in the dingy, tightly packed sixth district where none of her fancy customers would ever dream of going. If I followed the broad and winding road that spiralled out through all of Drachenburg's districts like the curl of a giant snail's shell, I would never reach it in time.

I ran through the smelly alleyways instead, cutting straight across the city. There were people in Drachenburg who were born, lived and died in just one district, and treated all the others like dangerous foreign countries. But to me every bit of it was home, from the sunny yellow first district at the city's heart, where the royal palace stood in unshakeable golden splendour, to the grimy, heaving fifteenth district, where even the king's soldiers hesitated to go. I'd learned a long time ago that the skinny, shadowy alleyways, tucked away like shameful secrets behind the houses in every district, were the secret veins of the city, connecting all the different neighbourhoods into a living, breathing whole.

I had to dart and skip from side to side as I ran to escape the disgusting run-off that gushed down the centres of those alleyways. Unfortunately for my fabulous outfit, there was no way to escape the smell. It had rained for the past week, so the gutters were bubbling and overflowing with a noxious, clumpy, dark liquid goo made up of rainwater mixed with leavings from chamber pots, horse droppings and rubbish. Even when I held my breath, I could feel the stench floating up to stick itself against my skin and clothes.

But it was worth it. Every time I leaped out from the end of another curving passageway, I emerged into a whole new world of colour, filled with different kinds of people, sights and smells. From the third district to the fourth, the fifth ...

There.

The big old brick warehouse hulked in front of me, all of the doors at the front propped open. No smoke was coming out of them, which was a definite relief. I didn't hear any screams yet either.

Good. I still had time.

I started for the closest door – and heard an all-too-familiar roar of rage.

Too late! I sprinted forward in panic.

The moment I raced through the door, I knew exactly where my best friend was standing, because everyone else was backing away from her in a widening semicircle. All the traders here were big, tough men and women, used to hauling around massive crates and competing for every sale of spices and ingredients from across the world, but at that moment, they all shuffled warily backwards in unison, their faces pointed away from me.

'*What* did you say about Marina?' roared a familiar voice beyond them.

Uh-oh.

If there was one thing all dragons were, it was territorial. No one was allowed to attack Aventurine's territory, which included not only the chocolate house itself but also Marina, Horst and me.

There were moments when I really, truly loved that fact. When I was lying awake late at night in my patchwork tent on the cold, bumpy ground of the riverbank, with the wind whistling through the thin cloth walls and a hundred other people shifting and rustling nearby, that knowledge – that no matter what might happen, I was part of Aventurine's territory now, and she would do absolutely anything to protect me, with teeth and claws and fire if necessary – filled me with wonder and a fierce gratitude.

Right now, though, was not one of those moments.

Right now was one of those moments when I wanted to scream at the top of my lungs while I shook some sense into my best friend's feral brain. Because sometimes dragons were *impossible*!

Taking a deep breath, I lowered my head, pushed my way hard through the closest knot of fully grown men and women and slipped out on the other side with a smile on my face.

'There you are!' I said to Aventurine.

At first, I couldn't even tell what had sent all those grown men and women backing away from her in fear. Oh, she was chock-full of seething ferociousness, of course. Her fists were clenched in front of her as she aimed a fiery glare with her unusual golden eyes at the man in the centre of the semicircle. And her new turquoise-and-orange dress was eye-wateringly garish enough to make *anyone* take a step back in horror ... not to mention the way her short black hair stuck out in all directions because she refused to ever take enough time away from the chocolate house to get a proper haircut ...

But really, she was barely five feet tall. What was their problem?

A flicker of movement on the wall behind her caught my eye, and I gulped.

Ohhh.

The *problem* would be the shadow that stretched behind my best friend's small, fierce, human body ... the shadow that grew larger and larger as I watched, spreading across the market stalls and the brick wall behind her, until it loomed over the entire market hall, with its massive tail lashing in anger and its giant jaws opening wide.

Even in shadow form, Aventurine's dragon teeth were impressive.

As an audible gasp of fear rippled through the crowd, I stepped forward, crossed my arms and gave her my sternest look – because I knew there was one thing that was even more important to Aventurine than territory.

'I hope you've got that sugar loaf for Marina,' I told her. 'She needs it *now* or else the new batch of chocolate will be completely ruined.'

'New ... what?' Aventurine blinked as if she were coming out of a daze. She swung around to stare at me, her shadow stretching, massive and reptilian, on the wall behind her. 'What are you talking about? We already made the new cakes of cooking chocolate today. And we don't put sugar in those anyway.'

'The chocolate creams then? Or hot chocolate?' I shrugged, keeping my expression bland. '*I'm* not the chocolate expert, am I? I don't know what she was talking about. But I know Marina was in a hurry, and *something* chocolatey is going to be ruined if you don't get back soon.'

Aventurine scowled, but I could tell that I'd won. Chocolate always won over everything, for her. Her shadow was already shrinking as she turned back to the big man who stood in the centre of the semicircle. 'I would have had it by now if *he* hadn't said –'

'And I'm sure he regrets it very much.' I gave the man a stern look. 'Would you like to give my friend a decent loaf of sugar this time? And maybe a partial refund, too, as an apology for the time she's had to waste in replacing that hollow loaf you sold Marina?'

For a moment, I thought he had actually seen sense. I watched his massive chest rise and fall in a shuddering breath. Then he looked past Aventurine. The dragon-shaped shadow was gone. Aventurine was only a twelve-year-old apprentice again, with short hair and an ugly dress. And I could actually see the shift in his perceptions as he glanced back at the other, watching traders ... and realised that he was only facing down two young girls after all.

His muscular arms crossed in front of him. His pale blue eyes narrowed and fixed on me. 'I think,' he said, 'that your friend's a public menace who's created a disturbance of the peace. Maybe we should summon the lord mayor's guard to deal with that.'

No, no, no! Panic started a drumbeat in my head as the traders around him rustled and muttered in agreement. Meanwhile, Aventurine let out a dangerous snarl.

The lord mayor hated our chocolate house and always had. Getting him involved now would be disastrous for everyone.

So I cocked my head, raised my eyebrows and asked the sugar trader gently, 'Are you sure that's a good idea? You do know whose protection she has, don't you?'

The sound that came out of his mouth then was almost as much of a snarl as Aventurine's had been. 'If you're talking about those *dragons* ...'

Oops.

The rustling and discussion around him disappeared as abruptly as if an alarm bell had sounded. Suddenly the whole market hall was dead silent and the tension in the air was unmistakeable.

Goosebumps prickled down my arms. *Not good.*

I knew this feeling in a crowd. I knew it much too well. After so many years of living on the riverbank, I'd learned to sense it in the air like a warning, because my community – 'the riff-raff on the riverbank, not even wanted in their own countries' – was always first to be blamed whenever things went wrong for the city as a whole.

And when frightened, angry people found a focus for their rage ...

Suddenly, they were all talking at once.

'Flying over our city like they own it!'

'Terrifying our children!'

'Who knows how long until they start eating *us*?'

'I heard the king's thinking of giving them human sacrifices, all laid out on the palace steps.'

'And you know where *those* will come from! Not from the fancy first district, oh no. They'll –'

'What are you talking about?' Aventurine yelled. She was panting as she stared around the semicircle of traders, her face creased in disbelief. 'Are you idiots? They're not going to hurt anybody! They're defending this city. They don't even eat humans any more!'

Ow, ow, ow. I cringed, but it was too late. Everyone was yelling now, and this time they all yelled the same thing:

14

'Any more?'

Never, ever let a dragon handle diplomacy.

I cleared my throat, putting on a desperate smile. 'If you'd all –'

But the sugar trader was already striding forward, his face flushing bright pink with fury as he pointed one beefy finger at Aventurine. 'Call me an idiot, will you? Well, we all know you're in league with those monsters! If you think you can –'

'Wait!' I yelped, and leaped in front of my friend. She growled, trying to get past me, but I kicked backwards, clipping her shin hard to stop her. 'Listen to me, everyone! I wasn't talking about the dragons!'

I was tall for a girl – and tall for my age, too – but I still had to tip back my head to look the sugar trader in the eyes. My chest grew tighter and tighter as the circle of angry traders closed in around us, leaving no way out.

Not again!

I *wouldn't* feel this helpless again. I had sworn that a long time ago.

I'd been seven years old the first time I'd felt that taste of sick danger in the air: the feeling of an angry crowd transforming into a mob. By then, I'd already lost my parents and any illusions of safety. I'd spent that long winter night shivering beside my brother and our neighbours, all of us crammed behind a protective wall of city guards, while raging local citizens burned down our tents and smashed our market tables in front of us, blaming that winter's food shortages on our arrival in their city.

But I wasn't that powerless little girl any more. I was *not*. I was the heroine of my own story, and I would make my story *work*.

If my first threat hadn't been intimidating enough then I only had one option left. There was just one person in Drachenburg who was more dangerous than any dragon.

'I was talking about the crown princess!' I said.

The traders around me all stopped moving. For the first time, I could see hesitation in the eyes of the man who led them.

There.

I took a deep breath and prayed for my best friend to stay silent. It was time to make up a really good story, *fast*.

CHAPTER 3

The sugar trader scowled. 'What about the crown princess?' he demanded.

If there was one thing I understood – one thing I'd spent the last six years learning – it was exactly how my city worked.

People in every district rolled their eyes at the lord mayor's vanity and his greed, as his new mansion in the third district grew more and more over the top, with new gold-plated furniture delivered every week. As for the king, he was liked well enough unless times were hard, and he was politely toasted on feast days ... but from the highest of the nobles to the poorest of the poor, no one trusted him to look out for their best interests.

Everyone loved the crown princess, though. She made certain of it.

It wasn't just that she was famous for speaking seven languages, or that she was the cleverest diplomat ever born into the royal family, winning allies and new trading partners from among our oldest enemies. That filled the merchants and the nobles with delight, as the coffers of the kingdom grew and the richest people in the kingdom grew even richer. But the crown princess didn't only look out for them.

She sent her own personal guard to the riverbank every year when the first blizzards came, carrying tinder and food and blankets to shield us against the cold.

And when the peasants on the northern nobles' estates had stopped their work in protest two years ago, their employers had demanded that the king send out his army, but the crown princess had visited the peasants to hear their stories first. Then she'd summoned the proudest and most influential of the nobles to a private conference at the royal palace. No one knew exactly what had been said there, but when those grand aristocrats came out again, looking stunned, a new decision was announced: all of their workers would be given pay rises for the first time in decades, along with real rights to their own land on the nobles' estates. All the newspapers had claimed to be astonished, but I wasn't surprised in the least.

She was the most powerful person in the kingdom, and she *always* knew the right thing to say. She'd been my idol for nearly all of my life – until I'd finally met her a few months ago and realised just how ruthless she could be.

No *one* became that powerful without being willing

to sacrifice other people along the way. She'd come very close to sacrificing my best friend's life in front of me when she'd thought it was necessary to save the city – and after I saw through her plans and saved Aventurine, I felt the full force of Princess Katrin's cold, calculating attention turn to me. It had been one of the most frightening moments of my life.

I never, ever wanted her to notice me again.

But I still understood the power her name carried in this city, so I took full advantage of it now as a new story spun into place in my head.

'Don't you think she has a plan?' I asked the trader. 'Do you really think she would have bargained with the dragons without knowing exactly how to handle them?'

'Well ...' His brows drew together. 'But the king –'

'I was there,' I told him truthfully. 'I watched her do all the real negotiations.'

'You?' A woman on my left let out a snort. 'What would a girl like *you* be doing near royalty?'

I drew myself up proudly. 'I work at the Chocolate Heart,' I said, 'whose fabulous and one-of-a-kind chocolate saved our whole city from the dragons' rage!' I heard Aventurine snort behind me, but I ignored it as I smiled brightly. 'You may have read our story in the handbills? Once the dragons tasted our chocolate, they gave up their thirst for blood and swore allegiance to the throne. The king himself has been our particular patron ever since we saved the city from ruin and made the most powerful allies Drachenburg has ever known.'

'Dragons ...' It was a hiss from nearby, and it could have come from any of the traders around me.

I didn't let it slow me down.

'That's right!' I said. 'We have dragons on our side now, which no other kingdom in the world can claim. And the crown princess has *me* to keep an eye on them! Why else do you think I'd be dressed like this? Have you ever seen any girl who looked like me?' I threw back my shoulders, showing off my masculine jacket. 'I'm her eyes and ears in this city. I can slip into any corner to bring her back the latest news. I can warn her of any danger that threatens, no matter how quietly her enemies try to whisper. Even the dragons like me now, because I bring them the chocolate they love. And I listen to everything they say. Honestly ...' I shook my head, *tsk*ing between my teeth in disappointment. 'Did you really think the crown princess *wouldn't* send a spy into their ranks, to report back everything she needs to know?'

The traders were whispering among each other now, forming narrow holes in their ranks – holes that were very nearly wide enough for a skinny girl to run through if she took them by surprise.

But I didn't budge. I didn't even blink.

Confidence was *everything*.

'You're just a girl,' the sugar trader said finally.

But I heard the uncertainty in his voice, and I let my smile deepen.

'Oh, really?' I raised my eyebrows and nodded towards the back wall, where Aventurine's shadow had risen to snarl at us all. 'And is my friend here just a girl? Really?'

All around me I heard air being sucked in past clenched teeth. My muscles tensed. If this went the wrong way ...

The first few traders stepped back.

'I always said the crown princess knew what she was doing,' said the woman who'd challenged me before.

'Can't get anything past her,' the woman's neighbour agreed. 'You remember how she tricked that ambassador from Villenne last year? Sent him home cursing and weeping into his wine. No one outwits our crown princess when it comes to negotiations.'

'The battle mages are probably in on the whole thing, too. You know they'll be working out how best to use the dragons.'

'And how to attack them if they ever turn against us!'

At that, Aventurine let out a low growl, but luckily no one was paying attention to her any more.

The tight circle around us had dissolved into clumps of two or three as traders on every side shifted and moved back, arguing and gossiping as they started back towards their stalls.

The market hall had been empty apart from the traders when I'd first arrived, during that slow period of early afternoon when all the restaurants in town were occupied with serving lunch. Now, a second round of apprentices started flooding through the doors with empty baskets, ready to pick up supplies for late-afternoon cakes, coffee and supper. Some of the apprentices were even younger than me and Aventurine, but they were all moving fast, their faces set in determination and their empty baskets slapping against their legs – because when you are lucky enough to have a real job in this city, you know the importance of a deadline.

If we didn't hurry, too, I would be late for our afternoon-rush shift at the Chocolate Heart, and Horst would worry himself into a stew. But I didn't let myself look impatient, even as I felt the clock ticking. Instead, I tilted back my head to give the sugar trader who'd started this mess my sweetest and most dangerous smile.

'So', I said, raising my eyebrows. 'Do I have to report this little incident to the crown princess, too?'

Dragons weren't the only ones who enjoyed winning battles.

Five minutes later, Aventurine and I were walking down the street with a fresh new sugar loaf *and* half a pound of vanilla pods, too. I laughed in delight as I scooped up one of the pods from the basket and tossed it up high into the air.

'Careful!' Aventurine caught the long, skinny pod in mid-air and tucked it neatly back into place. 'That's precious!'

'It was free', I reminded her, 'because of me. Aren't you impressed?'

'It was free because you're a menace', Aventurine told me. 'That ridiculous story!' Her face crinkled up as if she were in pain. 'I don't know which is worse – that you made them think my family were idiots or that they actually believed it! As if a dragon would ever swear allegiance to a throne!'

'My *brilliant* story saved us both.' I twirled in a happy, dizzy spiral, holding my hands out around me as I spun on the toes of my shining black boots. This street was beautifully broad, nothing like the narrow, stinking alleyways I'd raced through on my way here. I swept an elegant bow as I finished, as if Aventurine were a queen. 'You're the public menace, remember?'

'Pfft.' She snorted like a horse, striding past an open warehouse doorway and cutting off a group of people who'd been about to step outside, as if they didn't even exist in her vision. 'I didn't do anything to alarm them. Humans are –'

'*You* didn't have to do anything,' I told her as I gave an apologetic wave to the people we'd blocked. 'Not when you've got a thirty-foot shadow there to scare them for you.'

'Shadow?' Aventurine turned to frown at me. 'What are you talking about?'

'You were about to shift bodies,' I said. 'Everyone could see it.'

'Don't be stupid.' She scowled, her steps speeding up. 'I had perfect control.'

'Oh, really?' I skipped in front of her to hold her golden gaze. 'Then why was your shadow lashing its tail?'

Aventurine didn't say a word, but her scowl deepened.

'You've got to be more careful,' I said as I fell back into step beside her. 'Did you hear what they were saying about dragons back there?'

'I heard,' Aventurine muttered. 'But I don't want to talk about it.'

Well, of course she didn't. If it couldn't be fixed with chocolate or with violence, why would she be interested?

Unfortunately, I couldn't set the problem aside so easily. It kept twisting around in my head, casting a sickly pall over my victory, as we hurried from the grey, warehouse-filled sixth district into the bustling fifth district, where the house colours shifted to timbered black and white, and red-and-yellow flowers bloomed in all the windows. A clock was chiming in the distance, and I knew I'd have to work hard to calm Horst when we finally reached the Chocolate Heart, at least fifteen minutes later than I was due.

Horst would get over his annoyance once he understood the circumstances. But I clearly hadn't been paying enough attention. How could I not have noticed that people were worrying so much about the dragons? And why hadn't I predicted it in the first place?

If there was one thing I was supposed to be good at, it was riding the mood of my city. It kept me safe. It kept me strong.

From the moment I'd sneaked out of our family tent, while Dieter was sleeping, on our very first morning in Drachenburg all those years ago, I'd felt the whole city calling out to me – and it was exactly what I'd needed to put my broken pieces back together. Maybe our parents weren't here to protect us any more, and I would never again see the home I'd been born into ...

But every cobblestoned square and smelly corner of Drachenburg had been just waiting for me to come and make it my own, from the ancient tumbledown city walls that still circled the fourteenth district to the massive golden palace that sprawled across the city's centre, as unbreakable as a promise set in stone. There was a whole world beyond the riverbank, a world of colour and excitement, where no one ever seemed to be afraid.

I wanted it all. No, more than that: I *needed* it.

Dieter might think that the whole world revolved around our tiny market stall, but I had bigger dreams. I was getting ready to take charge of my own story, even if my older brother could never understand it ...

And the Chocolate Heart could *not* be the end of it.

I'd spent the last six years of my life living in patchwork tents on the riverbank, replacing one after another whenever a raging windstorm or a human riot stole the last one away from me. I was ready for a real home with walls that could never be broken or burned down again. That was why I'd turned down Horst's offer of a full-time job two months ago, even though the salary he'd offered had been dangerously tempting.

The Chocolate Heart had nearly gone out of business just before I'd got involved with it. The next time that Marina offended the wrong person, the whole shop could disappear, just like grains of sand swept away by the muddy brown river. I would *not* anchor myself to yet another home that could be taken away from me at any moment.

I had bigger plans ... or at least, I was supposed to.

How many hours *had* I spent working on those hand-bills when I should have been out roaming the city, searching for new and better opportunities?

How many times had I lingered in the Chocolate Heart after my official work was done, just hanging about the kitchen, washing dishes for free and sampling all the different kinds of chocolates that they made?

I wasn't a dragon, but I still had wings to stretch. I couldn't let myself get so distracted any more ... not even by the gorgeous smell of chocolate and a place that felt danger-ously like mine. *That* was a story I could never let myself believe.

Aventurine startled me, just as we reached the third district, by turning to give me a knowing look from her gleaming golden eyes. 'I can feel you chewing on your own scales,' she said. 'What are you worrying about now?'

'Me? Worry?' I snorted, putting an extra swing into my step, so that my scarlet coat-tails billowed magnificently around me. 'Why would I? I've got everything under control.'

And I almost believed it ...

Until the crown princess's soldiers came for me the next day.

CHAPTER 4

It was my least favourite day of the week: the day I worked at my family's market stall.

'Finally!' said Dieter when I arrived that morning.

Of course, I was a full three minutes early. I always was, every week, when I arrived for my promised shift. But I didn't argue. Why bother, when it came to my older brother? He'd only find something else to criticise – and I'd promised myself that morning, when I'd first woken up, that no matter what he said, I wouldn't let him under my skin.

Not this time.

So instead of pointing out the time on the massive clock tower that loomed in the distance, I smiled at him in exactly the way that I knew would annoy him most.

'Things to do, places to be,' I told him breezily as I slipped into place behind the rickety wooden table.

There was a snapping chill in the air, like a foretaste of winter on its way, and I rubbed my hands together for warmth as I ran an eye over the clothes stacked in front of me.

Then I raised my eyebrows just to torment him. 'Not much new since last week, is there?'

'Since I don't have anyone here to help me nowadays ...' He glowered at me through his spectacles as he refolded a twice-mended cotton shirt that had been left crumpled at the side of the stall by the last customers. 'I barely see you any more now that you've run off to play with those chocolate-making loons in the third district.'

Oh, I was *not* about to let that one pass! No *one* criticised my friends in front of me.

I crossed my arms and gave him a sweet, interrogating look. 'What exactly do you think is paying for our meals this week, Dieter, and putting savings for the future in our moneybag? Your little market stall? Or my work at the best chocolate house in Drachenburg, serving the king himself?'

'"Little market stall?"' New creases popped up in the shirt my brother was holding as his hands clenched.

I shrugged. 'Well? If you compare it to the Chocolate Heart –'

'This "little market stall" is the only inheritance our parents left us!' Dieter shook his head as he stared at me. 'Do you really not even care about that any more? Or ...' his voice dropped, '... about them?'

Oh. *Oh.* My stomach gave a sudden, sickly twist.

Dieter and I had fought plenty of times before. He wanted to keep me trapped where he could see me; I'd never been able to stay put. Over the last few years, I had started to feel as if we couldn't even speak to each other any more without leaving verbal bruises. Still, there were some words that neither of us had ever uttered.

He'd never dared make that accusation out loud, to my face, before. Blood roared into my ears, but I wouldn't let myself show any reaction. Not to him.

'Our parents wanted a better life for us,' I said quietly. 'That's why we got on that wagon train all those years ago. This market stall was just an accident of the friends they happened to make along the way.'

... Before we lost them.

But I never, *ever* let myself think about that. Not any more.

How could he?

'And now you're ready to throw it all away.' He shook his head, his thin face pinched in disapproval. 'Now that you've wormed your way into that fancy chocolate house so that you can use the people there –'

'Enough!' I grabbed the cold table with both hands, gripping it hard as I glared at him.

I hated that I could never stay calm with him any more.

I hated that I couldn't forget a time, long ago, when my big brother had looked at me with love instead of furious disapproval ... and when I'd clung to his hand for safety as our wagon had rolled into our new city in the dark.

Most of all, I hated everything I felt bubbling in my chest as his words sank like poison into my skin.

'So that you can use the people there ...'

I wasn't. I never would.

Was that what I was doing?

No. I wouldn't even think about that now, in front of him. And I would *not* give him the last word, no matter what.

'If you say one more word about the chocolate house *or* our parents,' I told him, 'I'm walking away right now. And I might not come back!'

My brother's jaw tightened, his tall, skinny body as rigid as a spike.

For a long moment, we stared at each other.

Then he took a deep breath, patted the shirt he'd been holding and set it down carefully.

'Next time,' Dieter said as he turned to walk away, 'try to wear something that won't scare off the customers. Like a *dress*.'

Argh! I had to stuff my hand into my mouth to hold back a scream of rage that would have followed him all the way off the riverside. I would not give him that victory ...

But I was shaking as I spun around, facing the back of the patchwork canopy that sheltered our market stall to hide my expression from the rest of the world.

'Once upon a time ...' I whispered to myself.

It was the way my mother had started all of her stories, every single evening of my childhood. Just the sound of those words had been enough, back then, to fill me with comfort as I'd lain safe and warm in my own bed, waiting to find out what would happen in someone else's exciting story.

Now I whispered the words to myself for strength.

I was calm. I was confident. I was the heroine of my own story, *not* the villain. And no matter what Dieter thought, our parents *would* be proud of me if they could see me now, travelling across the city every day to hunt down my own happy ending.

Hadn't they done the same thing all those years ago, when they'd bundled us into that wagon full of strangers in search of a better future? I was only standing here safely now because they'd been willing to take that risk for all our sakes.

I *would* succeed, just like they'd wanted. I'd fulfil all of their dreams by trying harder than ever – and no matter how much it might hurt, I would stop wasting so much time at the Chocolate Heart, pretending that it was my real home.

Even Dieter could tell that that wasn't true.

My throat tried to close up at the memory of his words, but I sucked in a deep breath and locked them away where they couldn't hurt me, along with the memory of my parents and the way I'd lost them all those years ago.

This was a new story for a new day. And I was determined to take charge of it.

Now.

Most people wouldn't have been able to hear the sounds of approach on the grassy riverbank, but I'd lived there for years, and my ears were attuned to every sound. So when I heard the creak of leather and the soft sound of footsteps on the grass behind me, I spun around with my best saleswoman's smile.

'The best clothing on the riverbank!' I said as I turned. 'And the cheapest prices ... ah?'

Two men and two women in silver-and-blue guards' uniforms stepped into place around my table, closing me in.

The one who stood directly in front of me put one hand on the hilt of his sword as he leaned across the piles of neatly folded second- and third-hand clothing, his dark eyes hard and fixed on me.

'Orders from the crown princess', he said. 'You're coming with us.'

Of course I tried to talk my way out of it. As soon as the first bright burst of shock faded, a dozen different explanations and excuses jostled for position on the tip of my tongue, each of them better than the last. But none of the crown princess's guards would listen to a word I said and, less than a minute later, I was being marched through the crowded river market like a criminal, leaving my family's market stall unattended and completely unprotected behind me.

If robbers stole our precious stock of clothing while

I was gone, Dieter would never forgive me. At least I'd managed to snatch up the moneybag from behind the table and stuff it into an inside pocket of my thick black jacket. But the thought of his expression when he came back to find our table empty and both me *and* our moneybag gone ...

I staggered, my chest burning as if I'd been knifed. The guard behind me forced me forward with a hard jerk of her knees, pushing me relentlessly ahead.

How could I have let this happen?

The guards had been so fast, hemming me in and marching me away before I could even try to run. Most people wouldn't have seen what happened. But the market was so crowded that *someone* out of all the traders in the stalls around ours must have witnessed it – so at least they could tell my brother I hadn't left our stall defenceless on purpose.

No, I'd been marched away by the crown princess's own guards ...

... So of course he would assume that I'd committed some unspeakable crime and been arrested for it.

I would have groaned if I could have forced any air through my lungs. But for once, my voice had completely deserted me. Dieter had always said it would get me into trouble one day.

How could I have been so stupid? Using the crown princess in my story yesterday in front of at least a dozen yammering traders ... how could I not have expected that she would hear about it?

Was it actually a crime to tell stories about her? Or to pretend to be working for her when I wasn't?

There had to be something I could say to make her forgive the insult. But no one was giving me any time to stop and think.

The guards' tall bodies closed me inside a tight, sweaty square as they marched in lockstep off the riverbank and on to the cobblestones beyond. I couldn't see past their broad shoulders in any direction, and no one outside the square could see me. At least that meant that none of the Chocolate Heart's customers would be scandalised by the sight of their waitress being marched off in disgrace to the palace to be lectured on her unforgivable impudence and then thrown into a grimy prison cell and ...

Wait.

Even in a panic, I still knew my city. We were definitely going the wrong way.

I poked the dark blue back of the guard in front of me. 'Hey! The palace is *that* way!'

He didn't even grunt in answer. But the woman on my left was smirking.

Uh-oh. I hadn't liked the idea of being marched off to the palace, but I liked this new turn even less ... especially when I realised, twenty minutes later, that we were marching into the grimy seventh district. What would the crown princess be doing *here*?

The guard in front of me unlocked the front door of a tall, sagging, wooden building that looked as if it might fall over any day now. The lightless staircase was too narrow for

34

the guards to keep their box formation around me, so they spread out, two in front and two behind, and kept me moving quickly up the creaking stairs.

Inside a building like this, there should have been dozens of families living in tiny, cramped flats, sending noise rocketing through the thin walls. But I didn't hear a single sound as we travelled higher and higher.

Someone had cleared this place out. And there was only one explanation I could think of: *someone* needed a safe place to hold meetings that no one else in the city could know about.

Or maybe ... a safe place to get rid of awkward people in secret?

My heart was beating as quickly as a hummingbird's wings, but I forced myself to take long, steady breaths as I climbed up the steep stairs in the dark.

If the crown princess wanted to execute me for my cockiness, she didn't need to do it in secret. She could have it done in the town square in the sunshine, and at least half of her nobles would applaud her for taking care of an uppity commoner. So ...

'Here.' The guard in front of me stepped off at the second-to-top landing and unlocked a nondescript door to one side. With a jerk of his head, he motioned me into the small, empty room beyond.

'What?' I raised my eyebrows at him. 'You mean I'm finally allowed to start walking by myself?'

His eyes narrowed. 'Go.'

'In a minute.' I started to straighten my jacket with care.

A hard shove from the guard behind me sent me staggering forward.

Catching myself on the open doorway with both hands, I said, 'I think I ought to take a moment first to –'

A second shove sent me tumbling into the room. I landed, sprawling, on a hard wooden floor as the door of the flat slammed shut behind me, leaving me alone ...

Or not.

'Well, well,' said a familiar voice as a second door opened on the opposite side of the room.

The most powerful woman in Drachenburg stepped inside. Her long, lavender silk skirts swished against the dusty wooden floor, only three feet from my outstretched hands. Her long black hair was swept up in an elegant, courtly style around her light brown face, leaving a few curls rippling stylishly around her neck. Her dark eyes were filled with sharp, dangerous intelligence ... and an amusement that made me burn.

The crown princess was smiling as she looked down at me on my hands and knees before her.

'You needn't kneel,' she said drily. 'Your name is Silke, isn't it?'

The panicked thrumming in my chest slowed down. Everything went still inside me as I suddenly saw myself from her perspective.

I would *not* let this pathetic moment be the end of my story. Not even if it meant my execution.

Never.

Taking a deep breath, I pushed myself up off the floor

and jumped to my feet with a wide, confident smile. I brushed the dust off my jacket with two quick swipes and then I swept an elaborate bow.

'Your Highness.' I tipped back my head to smile straight into her eyes. 'I assume that you need my help?'

CHAPTER 5

The crown princess's finely plucked eyebrows did not rise on her smooth brown forehead. The expression on her beautifully symmetrical face never altered.

But her whole, elegant figure went still for a moment, and I knew I had surprised her.

I took that moment to jerk my jacket straight with one quick twitch. I would have straightened the cravat around my neck, too, but without a mirror that was nearly impossible – and I didn't dare let her see me fumble.

So I locked my hands behind my back to hide their trembling and said calmly, 'I would have come if you had summoned me, Your Highness. You didn't need to send out your guards to bring me in.'

'No,' she agreed. Her famously rich, velvety voice filled

the room. 'Not if I had wanted you to know where you were going ... or to tell anyone else about our appointment.'

Uh-oh. My heart was starting to gallop again. But I wasn't weak or a victim, no matter how helplessly I'd been brought here. So I narrowed my eyes. 'The seventh district, you mean? In the block between Herrengasse and Margaretenstrasse?'

This time, her eyebrows did rise. 'I ordered that my tallest guards be sent, and that they not allow you any view of your surroundings.'

I threw my shoulders back and lifted my chin even higher. 'This is *my* city, Your Highness. I know every street of it.'

'I see.' A tiny, worrying smile tilted up the corners of her full lips. It didn't look friendly. It looked ... satisfied.

Had I just passed a test? Or failed one?

She didn't say anything more, so I finally added, 'And I wouldn't have told anyone if you'd asked me not to.' But my voice came out weaker than I'd wanted, and her lips curved into a full smirk.

'Not even in one of your infamous little handbills?' she asked. 'Or ... in a public marketplace perhaps?'

I *knew it.* My fingers clenched so tightly behind my back that pain stabbed down my forearms. I took a deep breath. 'Your Highness –'

But she interrupted me. 'This wasn't the first time you've pretended to work for me, was it?'

Wasn't it? I blinked rapidly, trying to remember.

'Four months ago ...' she prompted.

Oh. 'That's right.' I swallowed hard. 'That was how I got Aventurine in to see you when the dragons came.'

When Aventurine's family had first flown here to find her, the city had erupted with panic, certain that we were all about to be burned to the ground in a storm of dragon-fire. No one had wanted to let two young girls in to see the king and crown princess while they were in urgent confer-ence with their privy council – until I came up with exactly the right story to talk us past all the soldiers in our way.

'I ... I knew you would want to hear what she had to say.' I didn't like how small my voice sounded. *This is the wrong story.* I stiffened my shoulders and started again. 'Your Highness,' I said firmly, 'if you'd wanted to chastise me, you wouldn't have come all this way to do it. So perhaps you'd like to tell me, instead, what exactly I can do for you now.'

'Indeed.' Pursing her lips, the crown princess paced in a slow, considering circle around me, her silk skirts brushing gently against the floor.

I held myself still, my fingers tightly laced behind my back, as I felt her calculating gaze sweep across me from top to bottom.

'*Silke*,' she said, as if she were testing out my name. 'I've been wondering how best to make use of you for some time now.'

'You have?' The words came out as a squeak. Hastily, I cleared my throat. 'That is ... you have, Your Highness?'

'Oh yes. And I believe I've finally found the right moment. But it would be a ... considerable challenge.'

40

Her gaze rested on the spot near the right shoulder of my jacket where the cloth had been mended twice – once before I'd found it on our market stall, and once again afterwards, when the first, weak threads had snapped. I'd mended it in perfectly camouflaged black thread and neat, tiny stitches, but her gaze arrowed in on the imperfection, and I had to fight the impulse, too late, to cover it up.

'You're quick-thinking even when frightened,' she murmured, 'and you can talk your way around *almost* anyone ...'

Her eyes rose to meet mine, and my throat tightened at the silent message I read in them: I *would never be able to talk my way around her.*

'But,' the crown princess continued smoothly, 'can you pretend to be someone else entirely? And can you talk an entire court into believing it?'

'Your Highness?' I blinked.

She tilted her head to one side as she came to a halt at last, looking down on me again. 'What do you know about Elfenwald?' she asked.

And every ounce of my hard-fought calm dropped away as memories swept over me.

There was one story that I never told anyone.

It was a story I couldn't twist, no matter how desperately I wanted to.

It was a story without a happy ending for any of us.

Oh, Dieter and I got away, along with the rest of our wagon train. The horses pulled us out the other side of that terrible forest. Two weeks later, we finally arrived in Drachenburg and ended our long journey.

But my parents were left behind in the darkness.

And that story was set in Elfenwald.

I was only seven when it happened. I didn't know what was going on. But the wagon came to a sudden halt late one night, and I awoke to find that everything had changed.

Strange lights floated in the darkness all around us. The grown-ups had insisted that we drive through the night once we entered the kingdom of Elfenwald. They'd said it wasn't safe to stop in those green forests.

But I didn't see anything that looked unsafe. I loved the lights floating and shimmering in the air. They were *magic* – real magic, the kind I'd only heard about in my mother's stories! I couldn't understand why Dieter wasn't excited by them, too, or why his face looked so pinched and frightened in their faint, reflected glow.

I didn't even notice, at first, that my father was missing from our wagon, lost in the huddle of adults by the front, talking to someone I couldn't see.

But then my mother let out a cry of distress and stood up suddenly, sliding me off her lap. 'Dieter,' she said, 'look after Silke for a moment.'

And she was gone in a rustle of clothes in the darkness.

The grown-ups were all arguing now, their voices loud and angry and frightened.

It didn't matter how pretty the lights were any more. I wanted to find our parents, but Dieter wouldn't let me follow them. He was so bossy! I couldn't get past him, no matter how hard I tried ...

And then the magic lights all flickered out at once, and the flames in each of the wagon's torches vanished, too. In the sudden, shocked silence, a sweet, high laugh rang out in the pitch-black night. It sounded like the jingling of bells, and it came from every direction at once. Then the horses let out panicked whinnies, and our wagon suddenly hurtled forward again, while adults tumbled back into their places on every side in a panicked, noisy jumble in the dark.

Everyone was confused. Everyone was shouting. I couldn't spot my parents anywhere in the mass of shadows that surrounded me. No matter how loudly Dieter and I called for them, no one answered ...

And soon enough, we both realised the truth: they hadn't come back at all.

None of the other grown-ups would turn back the wagons, no matter how hard we begged over the next two weeks. They wouldn't even let us go back on our own. They caught us every time we tried to run away, until we had finally travelled so far that even Dieter said it was hopeless. We would never find our way back to our parents, no matter where they'd been imprisoned ... and the other grown-ups had simply abandoned them.

Oh, they felt guilty about it, I could tell – that was why they gave us the market stall when we arrived on the riverbank, in honour of our parents' memory, and why they protected it for us against the other adult traders.

But they wouldn't explain. They wouldn't even argue. They just whispered the word like a curse: 'Elfenwald.' I'd never told that story to anyone.

I looked into the crown princess's eyes, drowning.

But I didn't say a word.

'Nothing?' She arched one eyebrow, then shrugged gracefully. 'Well, never mind. I can hardly blame you. Their royal family lives underground, along with all of their court and most of their people. They only leave a few sentinels in the forested land above ground to protect their borders from intrusion. Unfortunately, those sentinels are more powerful than any of our battle mages. No one ever gets in or out of those woods without their permission, not even the cleverest of our spies.'

She didn't know.

She genuinely didn't know about my parents and our desperate trip through Elfenwald. I could see it in her face.

I drew a ragged breath, my shoulders starting to relax. But I couldn't let myself wait any longer.

Silke – that bright, confident girl without a past – wouldn't go silent. Not for this. She would be wild with curiosity, eager to collect new information. She would be a heroine searching for a bold new adventure, not a terrified little girl haunted by memories of floating lights in the dark.

Their *sentinels* ...

'They all live underground?' I repeated. I was proud of how smoothly my voice came out. It really sounded as if I were interested instead of secretly falling apart. I even managed to wrinkle up my face as if I were thinking about the question, as if this were the first I'd ever even heard of them. 'How do they make a living if they don't trade with other countries? They can't make everything they need without sunlight.'

'Oh, they trade,' said Princess Katrin. 'Their silver exports are famous across the continent – and we would give a great deal to become their favoured trading partners. But their silver is always sent through mysterious go-betweens, and they've never been open to negotiation. The royals themselves haven't even been glimpsed by outsiders for well over a century now.'

At that, I finally did discover some curiosity inside myself. 'What are they hiding from down there?'

'A fascinating question,' the crown princess told me, 'because their magic is rumoured to be unstoppable. According to history and legend, they have nothing to fear from any of us. But they've stayed locked within their hidden kingdom for over a hundred years ... which makes it all the more interesting,' she finished, 'that I've just received a personal letter from their royal family for the first time ever.'

She tapped one long brown finger gently on her skirt as her face hardened. 'It is,' she said, 'customary for royal invitations to be issued by a ruler's privy council, after months of deliberation and diplomacy, but the rulers of Elfenwald have announced their own imminent arrival at our court without waiting for any invitation from us.'

'Wait ...' My eyes widened. 'They're coming *here*?'

Her head inclined in a graceful nod. 'In five days, the royal family of Elfenwald will be visiting us for the first time in nearly two centuries "to re-establish our kingdoms' ancient friendship" – which is the first I've ever heard of any such relationship. And I've read a *great* deal of our kingdom's history. But you, Silke ...' Princess Katrin pinned me with her gaze. '*You* are going to help me find out what it is they actually want from us – and why they're suddenly so determined to insert themselves into our court.'

'*Me?*' I managed.

It was hardly even a word. It was a rasp from my throat, which had tightened until I could barely breathe through it.

I'd shut away my parents' story so many years ago.

I'd been so certain that I could never, ever change that ending.

'You,' the crown princess repeated. 'Didn't you tell all those traders why you'd make the perfect spy? You're too young to look dangerous. You're excellent at blending into your surroundings when you wish to. And, most importantly ...' her lips curled into a half-smile, '... you talk your way out of trouble and into other people's confidence in the most remarkable manner, as you proved to me yet again yesterday. Even the dragons trust you – and they have *never* trusted any human beings before! So ...'

She dropped her voice as she took a step closer, until not even the guards waiting outside could have overheard us. 'What I want,' she whispered, 'is for you to use that dangerously clever tongue of yours to talk the fairies into trusting you, too, so you can find out what they're *truly* after in my palace. If you can do it – if you can prove that you really are as good as you claim at blending into *any* group and bringing me back the secrets that I need – then you'll find a home in my palace, and a position in my service, for the rest of your life. No matter how long you live, you will *never* have to sleep on a riverbank again.'

A home in the palace and a position there *forever*? An hour ago, that promise would have been so far beyond my wildest dreams, I would have danced with joy at the very thought of it.

Nothing could ever break or burn those massive golden walls. Unlike the Chocolate Heart, Drachenburg's royal palace would never face the risk of closure. It was the one home in the world guaranteed not to blow away in the worst of storms.

But right now, that wasn't even what mattered most as my lips stretched into a dragon-fierce smile, my heart bursting with sudden, agonising hope.

'I'll do it,' I said. 'No matter what it takes!'

It was time to write a new ending to my family's story.

CHAPTER 6

'So *you're* going to be a princess?' Marina said two hours later. For once, her big hands stopped moving in the middle of her chocolate-making as she stared at me across the bright white kitchen of the Chocolate Heart.

Working at a nearby counter, Aventurine didn't even pause in her endless grinding of the cocoa nibs. Back and forth, back and forth ... It would have driven me wild with boredom after the first ten minutes, but when it came to chocolate, Aventurine never lost her patience. Still, she snorted at Marina's words. 'What's the point of being a princess?' she asked. 'I've seen the royals around here. They don't even have real crowns!'

'Oh yes, they do.' I cupped my hot chocolate in my hands as I sprawled back in my usual chair. 'Just because they don't choose to wear them everywhere they go ...'

'If you say so.' Aventurine shrugged. 'I've never seen them. Ever.'

Her disbelief hung in the air between us like a thick fog of dragonsmoke.

I rolled my eyes at her and took a long sip of fiery hot chocolate. The rich, dark taste of chocolate came first, and then a second burst of warmth from the chilli, lighting me up inside like a torch. I could do anything, powered with hot chocolate like this – but only if my best friend would stop being so awkward about it!

'It's called *good taste*,' I told her, 'and discretion. Dragons don't carry *their* hoards everywhere they go, do they?'

Aventurine looked at me sceptically over her grinding board. 'Are you telling me that princesses sleep on top of *their* crowns, too?'

'We-e-ell ...' An irresistible vision landed in my head: the elegant crown princess sleeping curled up like a dragon on a sharp bed of crowns, breathing out smoke through her perfect nose. I swallowed a laugh as I took another sip of my hot chocolate. 'I'm not saying it's *impossible*, but –'

'But we're wandering off the point.' Marina's hands were moving again, stirring her pot of chocolate cream with brisk efficiency, but there were tight white lines around the corner of her mouth that I had never seen before. 'Tell us exactly what that woman's talked you into doing.'

I should have known that Marina would be grumpy about my big adventure. She'd never thought much of royalty before. But I didn't let her bad mood dim the glow inside me as I crossed one booted ankle over the other and grinned at them both, willing them to enter into the fun of the story we were building.

I *had* to convince them before I faced Dieter. I had to know that someone was on my side.

'I'm not going to pretend to be a princess myself,' I told them. 'Just a country cousin and lady-in-waiting to the younger princess, Sofia.'

'Oh, *her*.' Aventurine folded the chocolate paste and re-rolled it. 'She writes letters back and forth with my brother about philosophy.'

'Really?' I blinked. 'I suppose we'll have plenty to talk about then, since we have friends in common.'

'I don't think so,' Aventurine said calmly. 'She doesn't like me at all.'

'*No!*' I made my mouth into a big 'O' of astonishment, clapping one hand to my face. 'I can't believe it!' Then I dropped the ruse and grinned at her, letting my hand fall back to my lap. 'Did you forget to tell her that you don't eat humans any more? Because you know that always reassures people *so* much.'

Aventurine didn't reply. But her golden eyes glinted as her lips curved into a smirk over her chocolate paste.

There was nothing that my best friend cared more about than chocolate ... and nothing she cared less about than being liked by anyone else.

Oddly enough, it was one of the things that I liked best about her.

'Anyway,' I said, 'I won't really be there to keep her company. I'll be there to make friends with her visitors and their ladies-in-waiting, so I can figure out what they all really want under the social niceties.'

I would do it, too. By the end of the royal visit, I would know everything there was to know about the mysterious royals of Elfenwald. It was what I'd been training for all my life, even if I hadn't realised it until now. I would be the perfect spy! I would blend in seamlessly and find out their secret purpose; I would reveal it to the crown princess and win myself a real home that could never be taken away from me ...

And I would finally find out, once and for all, what the fairies did with human intruders in their kingdom.

But I wasn't ready yet to share that part of my plan with anyone – not even the friends I trusted most in the entire world.

Marina and Aventurine would never want to hurt me, and nor would Horst; I knew *that* with every one of the instincts I'd developed over the years of surviving in this city. That was why, whenever I stepped into the kitchen of the Chocolate Heart, I could let myself relax and *be* myself for once, instead of shaping myself into something better for my audience.

It was why I'd fallen into the habit of spending far too much time at the Chocolate Heart in the first place.

But as much as I loved them, I also *knew* them, which meant that I knew exactly how hard-headed they could all be when it came to wispy emotional matters.

If Marina heard my plan ... I winced at the thought of it.

'*Do you really think ... ?*' she would begin in a tone that implied exactly how idiotic she thought I was being.

And Aventurine, of course, would just say it outright: '*You do know, by now, that your parents are probably –*'

No! I yanked my cup of hot chocolate up to hide my expression, sucking down a long, soothing gulp and squeezing my eyes tightly shut.

I wouldn't give *anyone* the chance to say that to me.

My parents were alive. They had to be!

They were locked up underground in Elfenwald, that was all, just waiting for someone to finally rescue them. For the first time in six years, it was actually possible – even a little bit *likely* – that that person might be me.

I wouldn't let anyone take that fragile new hope away from me.

So I lowered my hot chocolate cup and said brightly to my friends, 'You'll be there to see me do it!'

'We will?' Aventurine frowned. 'Are they coming here?'

'Don't be absurd.' I shook my head at her, sinking back into my chair and crossing one trousered leg over the other. 'You really don't understand the concept of royalty, do you? The Elfenwald delegation will be hosted in a wing of the palace itself. They'll be feasted and feted every day of their visit ... and ...' I spread out my hands in a generous arc, '... who better to make all the treats for the royal visitors than our own royals' favoured chocolatier?'

Marina groaned. 'Oh no.'

'Oh *yes*!' I told her with relish. 'The crown princess thought it was a marvellous idea! I've arranged everything for you already. You'll be given a chocolate kitchen in the palace for the entire week of the Elfenwald royals' visit. This is the highest honour any chocolatier in this city has *ever* been granted!'

'Lucky us,' Marina muttered into her chocolate pot.

'It *is* lucky,' I said firmly. 'Horst will tell you that. He'll be thrilled when he finds out!'

'I'm sure he will be,' she said sourly. 'And this all looks like a great favour the crown princess is doing us now, doesn't it?'

Something in her voice made me frown and look harder at her.

Marina was often grumpy, of course. That was just part of her personality, along with all of the softer parts inside that weren't so obvious to any new observer ... like the part that had led her to take as her apprentice a wild, half feral dragon-girl who'd been turned away by every other chocolate house in town ... and then had her welcoming me, a ragtag girl from the riverbank, with a kind of brusque, steadfast acceptance that I'd never known before.

In this city, only the wealthiest elite ever tasted chocolate – except in Marina's kitchen. Here, I'd been eating and drinking every fresh, chocolatey miracle she'd given me ever since the first day we'd met, and she had never once let me leave the shop hungry. Everyone else in this city sniffed and muttered about the untrustworthy 'ruffians on the riverbank', but Marina had shown me her trust by offering me a position in her shop. I might not have had a real home or family to vouch for me, but I was Aventurine's friend, and that had been good enough for her from the very beginning.

I would never stop feeling grateful for that.

So I couldn't dismiss her words, or the scowl on her face, as quickly as I would have liked. 'What are you talking about?' I said. 'This is going to spread the fame of the Chocolate Heart all the way out of Drachenburg. That's why I suggested it in the first place.'

It was the best gift I could think of to thank them for everything that they had done for me: the chance to become *so* famous that their business would be safe, at least for a while, after I left.

'Once newspapers all round the continent report that we catered the visit – I mean –' I winced – 'that *you* catered it – then for the next two years every tourist who arrives will want to visit the Chocolate Heart and make *your* chocolate a vital part of their Drachenburg experience.'

'That's not the part I'm worried about.' Marina's dark eyes pierced right through my shield of breezy confidence. 'How about *your* role in this little visit?' she asked. 'Sending a thirteen-year-old girl to spy on a set of visitors who frighten the life out of any adults with common sense ...' She shook her head, her face tight. 'I've heard horror stories about Elfenwald ever since I first moved to this continent. People who cross *those* borders don't come back. Don't tell me the crown princess is doing you any favours with this job! If I'd been in the room when she tried talking you into this kind of reckless, foolish danger –'

'I'm not afraid of them.' I made myself give a light, dismissive laugh.

Floating lights in the darkness …

No. That was a different world, in a different story, and we were safe in my city now. This was *my* story to control.

'It's a royal visit, not an invasion,' I said firmly. 'And besides, what could they possibly do to us? We have dragons protecting our city now.'

'Much use dragonfire against fairy magic,' Marina muttered.

Aventurine's mouth dropped open in outrage. 'My family would *eat* any fairies who tried to attack them with magic!'

'Like that food mage who turned you human?' Marina asked drily. 'What exactly happened to him? Remind me?'

'That was different.' Aventurine scowled. 'He tricked me into *drinking* his magic, and anyway, I wasn't fully grown. Magic just bounces off grown-up dragon scales when it's cast at them. That's why those stupid battle mages have never managed to hurt us.'

'Doesn't matter,' said Marina. 'Fairies aren't like battle mages. According to the stories, they won't do you the favour of attacking in a nice straight line out there in public with great sheets of noisy spells for everyone else to see. No, they're clever and they're tricky, and they work up close.' She looked at us both, her expression hard. 'Exactly how many dragons do you expect to squeeze inside that palace next week for protection?'

Oh. I saw Aventurine's gaze shutter even as I took a deep breath.

None of the adult dragons could possibly fit inside a human residence. It would never work.

'Never mind,' I said cheerfully as I lifted my hot chocolate cup once again to my lips. 'We don't need dragons anyway. It's only going to be a friendly visit.' I tipped my head back to swallow the last few drops of warm, chocolatey reassurance.

But my cup was empty. There was no hot chocolate left after all ...

Which meant I couldn't put off facing my brother any longer.

Dieter was waiting at the market stall when I got there. With twilight closing in around the riverbank, he was the only one of the traders who wasn't busily packing up for the day. Instead, he sat unmoving on the rickety stool behind our family table, which was still covered with neatly folded clothes. He didn't even seem to notice me when I stepped into view. His brooding gaze was fixed on some point in the distance as a damp, cold fog rose up from the muddy ground and wrapped itself around him.

I braced myself as I came to a halt fifteen feet away. My feet didn't want to move any closer.

Obviously, someone had told him about what had happened this morning.

It wasn't the first time I had seen him since then, of course. I'd dashed back to the market the moment I'd finished with the crown princess, my heart in my throat, just waiting to find out how many of our clothes had been stolen in my absence ...

But, astonishingly, not a single one had disappeared. The pair of married traders at the neighbouring stall had protected our wares for us. Frieda and Hanno didn't think much of me, but – like everyone else on the riverbank – they approved of Dieter.

What a pity that such a nice, hard-working young man should have such a shiftless, unreliable younger sister! They might not have said those words out loud, but their looks, as they'd told me how they'd kept our stall safe, had made their feelings perfectly clear.

That was all right. I hadn't thought much of them either, ever since that night when they'd left my parents behind in Elfenwald. But none of the adults on the riverbank even seemed to remember that any more. They'd probably buried that story even deeper than I had, in a locked box labelled *Survival*, and then just happily forgotten it so that they could sleep at night.

This morning, I'd turned away all of their suspicious questions and kept my place, almost dancing with impatience behind the table, until Dieter had returned at the very end of my shift. Then I'd fled before he could find out what had happened. I'd needed chocolate and company before I could face his reaction – and even now, with the last traces of chocolatey warmth lingering in my belly, I didn't feel anywhere near ready.

Never mind. I took a deep breath and stuck my hands

in the pockets of my silver trousers. *Time to get it over with and move on.*

Smiling broadly, I sauntered across the final patch of riverbank, between groups of traders busily dismantling their tables and tents. I ignored all of their disapproving glances and muttered comments as I called out to my brother.

'Having trouble?' I asked. 'If you've forgotten where everything goes, I can ...' *Ulp*. My throat closed up and wiped the smile from my face as he swung around to face me.

Dieter's face was stretched skeletally thin. The whites of his eyes looked huge. 'Marched away,' he said hollowly. 'By guards wearing the crown princess's uniform. *Arrested!*'

'Oh, that.' I tried to pull my smile back up, but it came out crooked under the weight of his stare. 'Yes, that probably did look bad, didn't it? But –'

'You talked your way out of it. Of course you did.' He shook his head, his face despairing. 'How many more times do you think that'll work, Silke? You're only *thirteen years old*, and you've already been arrested by the crown princess's guards! What's going to happen by the time you turn fourteen? Do you really think you can talk yourself out of trouble forever?'

My shoulders sagged as I sighed. The fog was rising higher now, licking at my knees and sending damp chills through my trousers. I shivered and moved closer, wishing I had more hot chocolate nearby.

'Look,' I said, 'I wasn't *really* arrested. It was just –'

'A misunderstanding?' Dieter groaned. 'Silke ...' Still

perched on his stool like a ragged crow, he closed his eyes against me. 'Are you even listening to yourself?'

'I am,' I said through gritted teeth, 'but *you aren't*. They weren't arresting me – they were *hiring* me. For a job!'

'A job?' He let out a half-laugh of disbelief. 'As a palace guard? *You?*'

'No!' I said. 'That's not it. But ...' I glanced round at all the traders nearby who were pretending not to listen. Frieda wasn't even pretending; she was leaning forward to hear us better, her pale green eyes narrowed with speculation. 'I can't explain,' I said, lowering my voice to a whisper, 'but you have to trust me. This is a good thing. For me *and* for us. I –'

'Never mind.' He let out a whooshing sigh as he slid down off the stool on to the muddy, fog-blanketed ground. 'Forget it.'

'Dieter ...' I frowned at him, thrown off balance. Shouldn't he have been yelling by now? 'I want to tell you everything,' I said. 'I really do. And I will, as soon as I can. But in the meantime –'

'I don't want to know.' The bitterness in his voice cut through my skin like a knife. 'But let me guess – you won't be coming back for your regular shift next week, will you?'

'Well ...' I swallowed, my throat dry. 'Not *next* week, no. I'll be busy next week. But what I'll be doing –'

'Won't be here.' His shoulders drew inwards as if he were protecting himself from some terrible menace I couldn't see. 'I understand.'

I started forward, reaching towards him for the first time in ages. 'Dieter –'

'No.' My brother gripped the table hard as he looked at me across the piles of second-hand clothes that had been his whole life for almost as long as I could remember. 'I meant it', he said stiffly. 'I don't want to know. In fact, I don't even want to hear your voice – because I can't trust a single word you say to me any more.'

Oh. Oh.

There was a rock sitting in my stomach. It was so heavy, I could barely breathe.

But I'd spent years learning how to put on a good face no matter how I felt inside. So I didn't let my expression shift as I nodded my agreement.

'Right', I said calmly. 'Well, then.'

Setting my chin high and whistling a jaunty tune, I turned and walked away, my heart hurting with every step … just like my older brother wanted.

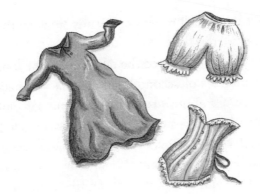

CHAPTER 7

I'd left both my family and the Chocolate Heart behind me, and there was a terrifying feeling of emptiness in my chest every time I let myself think about it. But I shoved that feeling aside every time, because there was a whole new world and a new story waiting for me in the glorious royal palace – and I was determined to discover every bit of it.

The palace sprawled all across the city centre, with its massive wings of golden stone stretching out in several different directions and opening on to squares and parks throughout the first district. There were even shops and restaurants built against some of its outer walls, like smaller creatures tucked together for warmth against the side of a colossal beast.

You could actually forget, on some of those busy

first-district streets, what lay behind the thick stone walls that rose above the cheerful shingled roofs of the shops. Then you'd turn a corner and be faced with sudden, overwhelming magnificence, as another wing of the palace opened up into a grand plaza, with ornamental fountains spurting high arcs of water, muscular statues reaching for the sky and the curving, window-studded lines of the palace itself rising at least three floors above the ground.

And every one of those floors was filled with secrets.

'What you have to remember,' the crown princess told me as she greeted me that first day, 'is that there are always more doors than you can see on first glance – and more people eavesdropping than you'd think.'

Well, that was less of a surprise than it might have been, after the way I'd been led into the palace in the first place.

I'd expected to be brought in through one of the busy, bustling servants' entrances that I'd passed hundreds of times before. Instead, the plain-clothed guard who was my escort led me into a tiny, cramped bookshop tucked into one of the palace's outer walls in one of the busiest streets in the first district. We walked past tables overflowing with books and pamphlets, we squeezed between towering bookcases that looked ready to topple at any moment, and then we slipped through a plain brown doorway at the back of the shop ... which led us into a darkened passageway, past a pair of watchful soldiers, up a narrow flight of steps, and through a final door into a room shaped like a hexagon, where the crown princess was waiting for us.

Five out of the six walls in the hexagon room were covered with giant paintings of bloody battles, each of them almost twice my height. There was just one small, wooden door set in the sixth wall, making the room look completely safe, closed-in and private ... but we'd stepped inside through the middle of one of the paintings themselves, which had a door sliced neatly into it to form a secret entrance. When we closed it behind us, only the lurid painting remained, and no one would ever have guessed what it was hiding.

I couldn't trust anything I saw in this palace.

Unfortunately, that included the guide that the crown princess had chosen for me.

'Sofia,' the crown princess said warmly when the younger princess stalked in through the wooden door to join us a moment later. 'May I present Silke? She's very kindly agreed to help us.'

'I know.' Princess Sofia pushed the door shut behind her with a thud. 'You don't have to introduce her to me as if she were a stranger, Katrin. She's served us both about a hundred times at the Chocolate Heart already ... which is why *this isn't going to work!*' Crossing her arms, she glowered up at her sister.

The crown princess's eyes hardened. 'Sofia ...'

'Everyone in court has been to that chocolate house by now,' Princess Sofia said flatly. 'They'll recognise her the moment they see her. It's not as if she ever faded into the background there!'

'And that past flamboyance is exactly why they *won't*

recognise her any more', the crown princess replied. 'What exactly do you think they noticed about her? Her perfectly ordinary features? Or the fact that she was scandalously dressed as a boy?'

'Ahem ...' I coughed politely into one hand.

I didn't think my features were *that* ordinary.

But the two sisters obviously hadn't heard me. They were too busy glaring at each other, inches apart, their faces set in identical expressions of frustration.

'You're telling me she can fit into the court?' Sofia demanded. 'Just look at her!' She waved at my outfit.

It was one of my nicest ones, actually – and one of my most discreet ensembles, too, in a deep, dark, forest green. I patted down the collar of my jacket reassuringly.

'She'll change her clothes.' All the warmth had fled from the crown princess's voice. Every word was a jagged white icicle, freezing the atmosphere as she did her best to stare down her younger sister. 'That is not a problem.'

'And the rest of it?' Sofia snorted. 'This is a visit of state, not a garden party. *Everyone* is going to be on their best behaviour. How good are all of her different curtseys, do you think?'

'They'll be excellent by the time you've finished teaching her', the crown princess snapped. 'Or you can forget about that order of books you just placed with the university in Villenne!'

Sofia didn't gasp or groan. But her eyes flared wide for a moment in unmistakeable outrage. Then she gave a sharp nod. 'Fine', she said. 'I'll teach her how to make her curtseys. But don't blame me when this all goes wrong!'

It wasn't the most promising beginning, to say the least.

But I was determined to make it work, so I kept a smile on my face as I followed Princess Sofia out of the room, ignoring the angry swish of her floor-length skirts as she stalked down the long blue-and-gold corridor.

Everyone in Drachenburg knew quite a lot about the two princesses. The crown princess was especially famous, of course, but almost anyone on the streets could have told you something about Sofia. Her age, for instance: twelve, which made her more than ten years younger than her older sister. Her height: a full foot shorter than Katrin's height at the same age, and about five inches shorter than me. Which parent she took after: her father – unfortunately for her, as everyone in the city agreed. And it wasn't only her father's infamous lack of patience that she had inherited.

Princess Sofia didn't have her father's reddish hair or pale complexion; like her sister, she had light brown skin, shaded in between their father's pinkish white and their late mother's deep, warm brown, and they both shared their mother's beautiful black, curling hair. But Sofia had the king's short, stocky build, square face and uptilted nose … and I recognised the scowl on her face as she strode down the corridor ahead of me, skirts swishing.

I'd seen that exact expression on the king's face whenever someone tried to interrupt him at his table in the Chocolate Heart to discuss politics when he was trying to focus on his chocolate.

Unfortunately, I didn't have any hot chocolate on hand to sweeten the princess's temper. So instead, I said, 'I hear you're a wonderful philosopher, Your Highness.'

'Here.' Without so much as a glance – she still hadn't looked directly at me – she turned and flung open a door on the right. 'You'll need to get changed before anyone else sees you.'

My eyes widened as I looked over her shoulder at the room beyond.

It was full of more maps than I had ever seen in my life. From the massive, colourful maps of the world that hung on the walls, each of them marked with clusters of silver pins, to the large globes placed all round the room – oh, and the dozens of rolled-up maps that stuck out from a nest of round holes in the big desk at the far end ...

Even more maps were unrolled and spread across that desk, and a colourful, tiled mosaic covered the floor, showing Drachenburg at its centre and all the other cities and kingdoms of the world spiralling out from it.

I'd never even heard of some of those places. But I could tell one thing immediately and for sure: this was the room of someone who wanted to control *all of them*.

'Well?' Sofia pointed at a small chair near the door, covered with a waterfall of bright colour. 'What are you waiting for?'

I hadn't even spotted the pile of clothing until then. But I started forward just as confidently as if I'd intended to do that all along ... and only realised my dilemma once I'd lifted the frothy, rose-coloured silk gown off the top of the pile.

Uh-oh.

Obviously, I knew how to put on a dress. Everyone knew how to put on a dress, even Aventurine.

But there were more things piled underneath this dress: strangely shaped white cotton things that billowed over the chair cushion, other cotton garments lined with hooks and even more things with long white laces trailing out of them ...

I'd never seen anything like them on the market stall. The women who shopped at the riverbank market didn't wear any frilly nonsense like this beneath their dresses, I was certain of that. But I wasn't certain of anything else. I didn't even know which fluttery garment I was supposed to put on first ... or how.

'Oh, for heaven's sake.' Sofia heaved a noisy sigh from the open doorway behind me. 'Are they not up to your high standards?' she demanded. 'You're only supposed to be a lady-in-waiting, you know. So if you were expecting something finer –'

'No,' I said. The word came out half strangled, as if the irony were physically choking me.

I'd never touched such fine clothing in my life. But I couldn't force myself to say any more about it, even though I knew I ought to be thinking up something flowery and complimentary to ingratiate myself. What could I possibly say when I didn't even know how to name any of the garments on the chair before me?

Suddenly, my nicest green outfit, so carefully chosen, felt as grubby as 'river trash' – the words I'd heard called out at me and my neighbours too many times to count over the years.

How had I ever thought I could carry off this charade? I *should never have left the riverbank.*

No. Stop! I closed my eyes and took a long, deep breath, fighting to still the panic rioting beneath my skin.

I was the heroine of my own story, and I would *not* be defeated even before it properly began. I was clever – I knew I was – and I'd been practising all my life at transformation. Anything I needed to know, I would simply find a way to learn, no matter how humiliating the price.

So I opened my eyes and turned around. When I met Princess Sofia's hostile gaze, I held it, even as my fingers clenched with the effort of forcing out the words I needed to say.

'I don't know how to put these on,' I told her. 'Will you please show me, Your Highness?'

Her eyebrows soared upwards. Her mouth opened. I braced myself for whatever scathing remark was about to come out of it.

She let the door fall shut behind her and started forward. 'Fine,' she muttered. 'I'll be your maid. But only this once!'

'Of course.' My spine felt brittle enough to snap, but I kept my face still as I unbuttoned my jacket. 'I'm a fast learner,' I told her quietly. 'I won't need to be told twice how to do this.'

'Why should you?' She snorted as she sorted through the pile of white underthings. 'You won't be doing it yourself ever again,' she told me. 'Haven't you ever heard of servants?'

'Um ...' My eyebrows rose as I bit back a sudden, unexpected choke of laughter. 'Your sister did tell you where I come from?'

'Oh.' Shockingly, she winced as if she were actually embarrassed. 'Well.' Looking away from me, she shook out a long white garment with a snap. 'From now on, you'll have a maid of your own who dresses you three times or more every day. You won't need to lift a finger. We can't let her see you wearing a coat and trousers beforehand, that's all.'

'I understand.' I finally relaxed enough to flash her a smile as I shrugged off my dark green jacket. 'Just ... don't let them be tossed away or burned, please? I do like these clothes.'

'If you say so.' From the tone of Sofia's voice, I could tell it was beyond her understanding ... but she didn't say anything else until a few minutes later, while she was lacing up a torture device called a 'corset' around my waist.

Standing behind me, her voice was almost too soft to hear. 'I could have done it, you know.'

'Sorry?' I started to twist around to look at her, but a jerk of her fingers on my laces forced me to stand still again.

'The spy work,' Sofia muttered. '*You* know. I told Katrin I could find out anything she needed to know. I *am* a philosopher, you know. It's not as if I'm unintelligent! I could actually be *useful* for once, if she'd only trust me. But –' she tugged viciously at my laces, and I gasped for breath – 'of course she didn't. She never does. That's why she hired you instead.'

Oh. Well, I might not be royalty, but I completely understood the difficulty of older siblings.

So I said, 'It doesn't all have to be me, Your Highness. We can work together! Then, if we succeed in the end, your sister will have to see –'

'I *beg your pardon!*'

The pressure at my back abruptly eased. The long ends of my corset laces fell free. A moment later, Princess Sofia was directly in front of me, somehow managing to glare down her nose even though I stood five inches taller than her.

'*You,*' she said coolly, 'will not discuss my sister with me, Silke – not now, or ever – because it is *not your place.*'

Ouch.

Apparently, we wouldn't be making friends.

I squared my shoulders despite the corset and stood at attention. 'No, Your Highness,' I murmured as meekly as possible. 'I only meant –'

'I. Don't. Care!' Sofia snapped. 'You can be as charming as you want, since you're *sooo* good at it, according to Katrin. You can flatter me all day long, for all the good it'll do you. But none of it will ever make a difference, because you – *you!* – are the person my sister chose over me. And I will *never* forget that or forgive you for it. Do you understand?'

My eyes widened. 'I ...'

'*Do you understand?*' she repeated in a near bellow.

At that, I dropped my gaze like a good, submissive servant. 'Yes, Your Highness,' I said. 'I do.'

And I did.

This mission was going to be even more difficult than I had imagined.

CHAPTER 8

Over the next four days, I figured out one thing for certain: I hated pretending to be a lady.

Oh, it wasn't the corsets or the curtseys – I learned how to manage all of those quickly enough. Within less than a day, I'd mastered the slow, gliding walk that all proper ladies needed in order to move about safely with layers and layers of cotton and silk swishing dangerously about our ankles. Ladies never ran – because, as I discovered, they *couldn't*. Their beautiful, expensive gowns would trip them up if they ever dared to try.

The other ladies-in-waiting weren't a problem either. Anja and Lena, two twelve-year-old cousins, were giggly, good-hearted and bursting with boredom in the younger princess's quiet apartments, so they found it the best new game in ages to teach an unpolished country girl like me how to behave in a royal palace. Proper Ulrike – the oldest and most perfectly correct at seventeen – kept herself at a superior distance from the rest of us ... but even she unbent the first time I told a really good story to make the endless, dragging afternoon hours pass a little quicker for everyone.

It was one of the best stories I'd come up with over the years, with a brave, strong girl daring everything to save her family, and after all the nights I'd spent telling it to myself before falling asleep on the riverbank, I knew exactly how to tell it well. All three of them had gathered close about me by the end of it, while Princess Sofia pointedly kept her nose stuck in a book at the other end of her beautiful green-and-gold salon, and a tall grandfather clock ticked with agonising slowness in one corner.

'But what about the youngest prince?' Lena asked, wide-eyed. 'He still had one arm turned into a swan wing. What happened to him afterwards?'

'He certainly couldn't have made a very good marriage.' Ulrike frowned thoughtfully. 'Although, perhaps, if –'

'Hmmph.' Princess Sofia slammed her book shut and stalked towards her bedroom. 'What nonsense!'

But even Sofia herself wasn't the worst of it.

The real problem was that the palace walls – so strong and so wonderfully, perfectly safe – felt as if they were closing in around me like a noose – a noose that tightened more and more with every minute I spent being a proper lady inside them.

Because I was a lady, I was laced by a maid into a new dress every few hours, with different colours and styles for different times of the day. There was just one thing that all of those fancy, tightly corseted outfits had in common: they were all designed to make girls look pretty and *stand still*.

The princess herself had lessons in statecraft and foreign languages and a dozen other intriguing subjects to occupy her, but she didn't share any of those with us. Instead, she retreated to a private room with her tutors for hours every morning and afternoon, leaving me with nothing to do but sit and smile with the other three ladies-in-waiting in our colourful silk gowns, like butterflies trapped in a cage for Princess Sofia's entertainment.

Ulrike embroidered and wrote letters to pass the hours. Anja and Lena played everlasting games of cards and Twenty Questions.

I sat with them, I smiled, I kept my feet and hands still, and I tried with all of my might to keep myself from exploding in one big, sloppy, colourful burst of perfectly unladylike frustration.

Blend in, I chanted to myself. *Blend in! You told the crown princess you could do it.*

My gaze slid yearningly, again and again, towards the closed door that led out to the rest of the grand palace … but I never made a move towards it, because in my new life I couldn't.

I was a lady-in-waiting. I *waited* upon my employer's pleasure every day.

But in the middle of my second night, I lost my self-control completely.

I was lying there in that big, stuffy bedroom I shared with Anja, Lena and Ulrike, all snoring quietly on their own soft, cushioned beds.

In the darkness, there wasn't a single distraction to save me.

There was no wind blowing through any thin tent fabric here; no rocks or bumps beneath my back. I should have been sound asleep like the others, enjoying the decadent luxury of a real mattress underneath me. But my entire body was wild with desperation, and every muscle I had was clenched. If I didn't escape now, I wouldn't make it through even one more day in Sofia's stifling apartments.

I slid out of bed before I could think better of it, and I hurried across the carpeted floor on bare feet, holding my breath the whole way.

If the crown princess ever found out what I was doing ... If *Sofia* found out and told her ... !

This wasn't part of my job description, no matter how hard I tried to twist it. Even I couldn't think of any excuse to sneak around in the middle of the night like a thief. But ...

No one will catch me, I promised myself as I tiptoed into the grand salon, shrouded now in utter darkness.

I knew exactly where to go.

The walls of the salon were hung with silk wallpaper

in rich golden and green vertical stripes. Every single stripe was perfectly even and exactly the same width as all of the others ... except for one.

I'd taken careful note of that stripe that afternoon as I'd sat obediently still on the couch for hours. I'd remembered the entryway hidden in the hexagon room's painting, and I'd memorised that spot on the salon wall until I could find it by heart without any light required.

When I pressed my hand against it now, I heard a creak that told me I'd been right. The wall shifted against my hand. A door fell open into deeper darkness.

I *was free*.

I took my first real breath in ages as I stepped from the lushly carpeted salon into a narrow, hidden corridor, my feet landing on bare wood.

Finally!

I already knew every inch of my city. Soon, I would know every inch of my new home, too.

And then, maybe, I wouldn't feel so stupidly desperate to escape it any more.

Long after the other girls fell asleep in their beds, I explored the palace in the dark, flitting like a moth in my long, pale nightdress through the narrow servants' corridors that ran behind the grand rooms.

That night and the next two nights, I pressed my hands against panel after panel to search out all of the secret passageways. I memorised the location of every posted guard. By the end of my second night of explorations, I had almost forgotten what it really felt like to step outside in the open air, but I had a map of over half of the massive palace in my head.

It was enough. At least it meant that I could get out if I needed to. Remembering that helped me breathe through my endless, elegant, ladylike days...

And then, on my third night of investigations, I found something different. I was wandering through the corridor that ran behind the first floor of the south-west wing, trailing my fingers along the narrow walls beside me, when I suddenly smelt it.

Chocolate. Unmistakeable!

It was a twisting, curling scent in the air, elusive and irresistible, and it grew stronger and stronger as I chased it, moving faster and faster until I was nearly running. I followed that smell down a narrow staircase that I had never seen before, and I found myself standing just outside a small room far from any of the huge, bustling main palace kitchens. The door was half propped open to let out chocolate-scented steam. Candlelight drifted out from the room, too, along with a familiar clattering of pans ... and the murmuring of two voices I immediately recognised.

Marina and Horst!

I took a step closer, drawn in like a moth to a lantern.

Then a sudden, loud snore broke through their harmony of voices, ending with a sputter and a growl.

There was a moment of silence. Then two low, affectionate laughs sounded in unison.

'Shh,' Marina murmured. 'Even fierce dragons do get worn out now and then, after all.'

Their voices dropped into indecipherable whispers.

So this was where the crown princess had put the chocolate kitchen for the duration of the fairies' visit! Aventurine was sleeping in there just as she slept in the kitchen of the Chocolate Heart, while Marina did some late-night cooking to calm her nerves and Horst kept her company as he often did, the two of them quietly talking over the events of the day.

I could imagine the warmth and cosiness in there so well, it physically *hurt* – and at that moment, it welled up inside me like a wave, threatening to wash away all of my careful years of planning.

I could sleep in there *so* much more easily than in my airless room upstairs! Curled up on the floor beside my best friend, surrounded by warmth and chocolate and everyone in the world who loved *me*, Silke – not just some clever story I'd made up so that other people would like me ...

I wouldn't just sleep. I would *rest* as fully as I'd let myself rest years ago, the last time I had felt truly safe ...

And *that* was the problem.

It would only be an illusion of safety now, just as it had been all those years ago. The people who loved you *couldn't* provide real safety, no matter how much they might try. No matter what it took, I would not let myself fall into the trap of believing that kind of promise ever again.

Losing it last time had nearly shattered me.

No, the only real safety I would ever find – the kind that I'd dreamed of and worked towards – was waiting upstairs in my stuffy bedroom in Sofia's grand wing of the palace, full of rich silk and carefully guarded wealth, with armed guards stationed outside to protect us.

That was where I belonged. It was the life I had *chosen*.

But if I walked into the chocolate kitchen right now, I knew I would never be able to make myself leave again.

Tipping my head forward, I drew in a long, deep, chocolate-scented breath, closing my eyes to absorb every last trace. That luscious warmth, that rich sweetness and comfort, and even that dangerous tickle at my heart that whispered, Home ...

I let myself savour it all for one delicious moment.

Then I turned and ran up the steps of the hidden staircase in the dark before I could be a fool and give up everything that really mattered.

I ran all the way through the darkened servants' corridors until I reached Sofia's apartments, and then I sped directly to my bed without letting myself turn and look back even once. I tucked myself in so tightly under my feather-filled duvet that I could barely move, and then I stared, panting, into the darkness overhead.

The other three girls were snoring quietly. The thick mattress beneath me and the velvet-lined covers around me were warm and lush and all enveloping.

I'm going to win myself a real place here forever, I promised myself. *By the end, no one will ever imagine I don't belong here.*

Not even me.

I closed my eyes, gripping the duvet tightly, and then I finally fell asleep, with the smell of chocolate floating tauntingly through my dreams.

CHAPTER 9

The next morning, it was time to meet the fairies.

Stepping out of the royal apartments during daylight should have felt like escaping from a cage. But as I glided through the long galleries and broad, open corridors with the other ladies-in-waiting, in our rustling gowns and petticoats, my head felt stuffed full of fog and dreams and my heartbeat thudded in my ears.

Elfenwald. The name breathed through me, leaving behind the distant echo of poisonously sweet, high-pitched bells. Fairy laughter. I had never forgotten that beautiful, terrible sound. I still heard it in my worst nightmares.

After all these years, I was about to come face-to-face with the creatures who had stolen my parents from me.

Waves of blood rushed up and down my arms, leaving

my fingertips tingling and goosebumps scattered in their wake.

I wanted to run, but my long skirts wouldn't let me. I laced my hands in front of my stomach and squeezed my fingers so tightly together that they burned.

It wasn't enough to let the whirling energy out.

There was just one moment, when we passed a line of narrow windows that looked out over a bustling square, when I lost my focus for an instant. It was so strange to see the life of the city outside continuing just as it had before I'd moved here, all those busy people completely unaware of what was happening in the closed-off world of the palace.

There was even a light shimmer of snow falling outside. When had it started snowing? I'd been stuck inside Sofia's stuffy rooms for so long, I'd almost forgotten that there was such a thing as changing weather in the outside world.

A group of adult courtiers stopped to bow low in our direction, and I wrenched my gaze away from the window to smile and nod in return. If Dieter could have seen me accepting their bows as my due, he wouldn't have believed his eyes. I really *did* fit into the royal court, at least on the outside. I'd transformed myself into a lady.

But I couldn't stop my tightly laced fingers from trembling as I followed Sofia and her stern-faced honour guard of soldiers into the grand gallery where the court was gathering to await our visitors.

Sweat and perfume filled the warm air. Nobles made

way for Sofia in rippling waves of respectful bows and curtseys, and we ladies-in-waiting swept past all of them, following our princess across the tiled floor to where the king and the crown princess stood with their own entourages assembled behind them.

A high, arched ceiling rose overhead, painted with magnificent white clouds, a bright blue sky and portraits of past kings gesturing graciously down at us. Tall, skinny windows lined the wall on our right, framing a courtyard full of statues and softly falling snow.

As we took our places, four muscular footmen stepped to the giant wooden doors before us and began to heave them open.

Now.

My breath stuck in my throat with sudden, choking panic.

This was really happening.

Elfenwald ...

Frantically, I tried to capture a memory of my parents' faces, to keep my feet anchored solidly in place despite the voice in my head that whispered: *Run.* But it had been too many years since I had seen them; I couldn't put the pieces together any more. All I had left was the echo of their voices and a vague memory of how they'd *felt* to me as a child: my father's warmth; the comfort of my mother's stories washing over me before bed every night ... I clung to those fragmented memories with all of my might.

I *won't leave without you,* I promised silently. *Not this time.*

A sliver-thin crack opened between the doors. The footmen panted with effort.

The crowd behind us rustled with anticipation.

'What's taking them so long?' Anja whispered behind me as another two footmen hurried over to help the first four. 'Those doors were never *that* heavy before!'

Something sparkled and blurred between the doors, almost too faint for me to see. I blinked rapidly, trying to clear my eyes. It couldn't be ... !

But it was.

Three balls of wickedly sparkling golden light slipped between the slowly opening doors and hovered in mid-air ten feet in front of them, turning and bobbing in place.

I had to clench my teeth together to stop them from chattering. I'd wanted to meet the creatures who had stolen my parents? Well, here they were. *Exactly* the way I'd remembered them!

A scream rose up through my chest, but I pressed my lips together, swallowing it back down with grim determination. I *would not* let them win.

How could I remember these golden nightmares more vividly than I remembered my own parents?

Dozens more lights followed the first three through the gap and clustered together in a tumbling, shifting group.

Gasps of wonder echoed around the room.

I remembered feeling that wonder, once. That night in the darkness of the Elfenwald forest, I'd laughed and reached out to those lovely, beckoning lights even as the adults' voices grew angrier and more frightened, until ...

I set my jaw hard, yanking my gaze away from them. My beautiful, expensive skirts were crumpling in my grip.

I wouldn't show them any fear. I *would not.*

Beyond the lights, through the slowly widening gap between the doors, I saw a deep-green darkness where there should have been a large, airy waiting room full of sunlight.

I knew that darkness in my bones, just as I knew the kinds of trees that rustled within it, even though it had been six years since I'd last seen them.

I couldn't breathe.

A high, fluted melody sounded in the distance. The golden lights shot forward in a shimmering cloud, weaving in and out among the crowd, as courtiers turned round to watch them go.

The massive doors flew open with a crash that sent the big, muscled palace footmen stumbling out of the way.

Light flared from the open doorway, blinding me. Something brushed against the back of my head. I jumped, twisted round – and threw my hands up in self-protection. 'Ahh!'

Silver, diamonds, rubies and more showered from the painted ceiling in a glittering cascade of necklaces, chains, circlets, rings and bracelets.

'It's a miracle!' Lena gasped beside me. 'How –?'

'Who *cares* how?' Anja demanded, lunging forward. 'Just *catch* them, for goodness' sake!'

It was a fortune beyond imagination, a dragon's hoard of jewellery and precious gems falling through the air around us. As the first shock passed, Drachenburg's highest nobility turned into a mob of unruly children, leaping and knocking into one another as they each sought to grab the sparkliest, shiniest pieces for themselves.

It was overwhelming. It was chaos. In the midst of it all, in the corner of my vision, I thought I glimpsed something hurrying past, a blur of red low to the ground ... but before I could even blink to focus, a middle-aged nobleman leaped between me and whatever-it-was in pursuit of a ruby choker.

Beside me, Lena and Anja giggled helplessly as they spun around in dizzy circles, grabbing out for everything they could catch. Ulrike's eyes narrowed with concentration as she snatched one piece after another from the air with grim accuracy. But Sofia stood still, her hands clenched by her sides, watching it all with an unreadable expression.

Even the smallest of those bracelets could have paid for months of food and firewood for both me and Dieter. If I *caught fifteen or twenty ...*

A silver and sapphire necklace landed on my shoulder. I lurched back, shaking it off as if it were a venomous snake.

I didn't want any shining fairy promises.

Not after last time.

'*Our friends!*' A woman's voice rang out through the hall.

I hadn't even heard the fairies coming.

Suddenly, the open doorway was full of more than a dozen people dressed in magnificent, multicoloured, brocaded robes and elaborate, exotic hairstyles – and every one of them glowed as if they had internal fires rising from deep within their bodies.

It was astonishing. It was so eerie, it made the skin all over my body prickle. It was *magic*, inhuman and unmistakeable in the midst of our cheerful, brightly painted great hall.

They were so full of magic it was *spilling out through their skin*. No wonder they didn't mind living underground! They must see in the dark better than cats.

And all these years my parents had been trapped beneath the ground with these glowing people-lamps as their captors.

'Our *dear* friends.' The tall and shining woman in their centre stepped towards us, smiling and holding out her hands as if she were the hostess here, not Princess Katrin.

If she hadn't been holding my parents prisoner, I might have found the fairy queen beautiful. Her deep auburn hair was drawn up into a sparkling black net above her long, pale throat. As she glided forward to meet our royals, her black and purple robes swished in graceful folds around her, golden embroidery glimmering in their edges. The whites of her eyes sent off sparks like diamonds in the sun, and her lips curled into a strangely familiar smile.

Oh! I sucked in a breath. I knew that smile.

It was the expression every sleek, prowling street cat

in Drachenburg wore when they caught hold of a fat mouse's tail. It was their look of anticipation as they prepared to play with a new victim – but only until they grew bored enough to pounce in for the kill.

'Your Majesties.' The crown princess stepped forward to meet her counterpart, and the whole room bustled into action.

Finally.

Along with every other human girl and woman, I swept out my skirts and sank into a deep, respectful curtsey. I'd practised my curtseys so much over the last several days that I didn't even need to glance down to keep my feet from tangling in my petticoats.

My proper mission was beginning at last.

'Queen Clothilde,' the crown princess said. 'King Casimir.' She nodded to the tall, lean man who stood behind the queen, glowing and elegant, with long, loose waves of jet-black hair falling around his light brown cheeks. 'Prince Franz and Prince Ludolph.' She nodded graciously to two teenaged boys who lounged casually beside their father, looking like desperately bored, glowing statues with sharper-than-usual cheekbones. 'We welcome our honoured visitors to Drachenburg. May this be the first of many such visits.'

'Indeed.' While her husband inclined his head with an enigmatic smile, Queen Clothilde took a quick stride forward, waving one pale hand to indicate the room. 'We do hope you will all accept these paltry, insignificant little tokens of our appreciation for your kind hospitality.'

Her gaze rested on a nearby courtier, who was clutching a pile of priceless fairy jewellery against his chest. Her smile deepened. 'This is, of course, only the tiniest fraction of the rewards any allies of our kingdom may expect to receive in the future.'

A sigh of wonder rippled across the room.

The crown princess's eyebrows rose infinitesimally.

My teeth set together.

Don't listen to her! I tried to beam the message across to my royal employer. *She's trying to bribe you. But for what?*

Princess Katrin's tone was serene, even as her courtiers rustled and whispered with excitement. 'We certainly hope to come to an agreement that will benefit us both.'

'Of course, of course. Why, I'm certain your little kingdom has many advantages – at least, to one who knows how to make proper use of them.' The fairy queen's smirk made my spine prickle up and down in warning. 'But as charming as this little reception is …' She turned pointedly to look across the gathered nobility of Drachenburg in all their splendour. Then she let out a theatrically disappointed sigh. 'I must confess, this isn't *quite* what we were hoping to see when we arrived.'

'I beg your pardon?' Princess Katrin's narrow eyebrows rose, her expression chilling. 'Is there something in particular you were expecting from us, Queen Clothilde?'

The fairy queen's voice was as sweet as an over-sugared chocolate fancy. 'Well, naturally we were *expecting* to meet your famous dragons. Haven't you been bragging insufferably about them to the world? Or was *that* fabled alliance only another lie, just like so many other past human pronouncements?'

'A lie? What? *Bragging?*' King Leopold's face reddened as he stepped up to his eldest daughter's side. 'I don't know what you mean by *that* remark, Your Majesty, but whatever rumours have been flying about underground, I can tell *you* –'

Snap! The fairy queen clicked her long, elegant fingers together. Emerald-green smoke puffed above her white, glowing palm ... and an all-too-familiar piece of paper appeared above it.

King Leopold stumbled to a halt, eyes widening.

'You see?' Queen Clothilde waved the handbill triumphantly.

Its headline stood out in unmistakable, giant print:

CHOCOLATE SO SWEET, IT BROKERED A BRILLIANT TREATY.

Oops.

'We know everything!' she declared.

The fairy king nodded gently.

The two fairy princes smirked.

Sofia looked positively murderous.

Oh, mud! I swallowed a groan as the crown princess turned to give me a meaningful look.

At least now I knew that *someone* had been reading my handbills!

CHAPTER 10

'Well?' the fairy queen demanded. 'Where *are* your famous dragons then? Hiding in the cupboards perhaps? Or ...' she arched one glittering auburn eyebrow, 'have they somehow turned invisible?'

Her sons both sniggered.

King Leopold's broad pink face turned even pinker with outrage. 'We don't keep them as pets about the palace, y'know!'

Oh, *ouch.* Thank goodness the chocolate kitchen was well out of earshot! If Aventurine had overheard that line ...

'Ahem.' Princess Katrin cleared her throat. 'I'm afraid our respected allies have other commitments this week, so, regretfully, they cannot share in the pleasure of your visit.'

Ha. That was definitely royal-speak for: 'I *am far too*

clever to invite a bunch of fire-breathing dragons to a delicate diplomatic event!'

'Hmm.' Queen Clothilde narrowed her eyes. '"Respected allies", you say? And yet, in all of our long history, there has never been any instance of those feral beasts forming political alliances with *anyone.*'

Behind her, her husband spoke for the first time, his voice deep and gentle. 'You must understand,' he murmured, 'that truth is *extremely* important to our people.'

'Of course.' Princess Katrin smiled graciously. 'And now –'

Queen Clothilde spoke over her, snapping out the words like bullets. 'We could never enter into an alliance with any rulers who lie to us. *Ever!*'

Sofia's face scrunched into a scowl of pure fury.

Her older sister gave the fairy queen a long, meaningful look. When Princess Katrin finally spoke, her voice was perfectly measured. 'I am certain,' she said, 'that lies will not be a problem ... on *either* side of our negotiations.'

She turned to her sister. As if by magic, Sofia's scowl disappeared, replaced by a forced smile.

The crown princess smiled back at her approvingly. 'Let us lead our honoured guests to their banquet now, to refresh them after their long journey. But perhaps ...' Katrin tilted her head, as if suddenly struck by a new idea, 'you might send one of your ladies-in-waiting to order up chocolate for us to enjoy in my private parlour afterwards?'

Aha. Even Sofia couldn't pretend to misunderstand

which lady-in-waiting her sister meant for that task – and even Sofia didn't dare disobey the crown princess in public.

Sighing, the younger princess turned to me and nodded.

I curtseyed and ducked my head submissively – *nothing to see here, oh no, nothing suspicious at all* – as I hurried away through the crowd of jostling courtiers, leaving the fairies and their sinister golden sentinels safely behind me.

Phew.

The smell of cooking chocolate a few minutes later, as I slipped through a hidden panel into the servants' corridor closest to Marina's kitchen, eased the tension in my shoulders even more. As I followed that rich, delicious scent, my feet moved faster and faster of their own accord, until I had to lift my skirts to an unladylike height just to keep from tumbling down that narrow staircase that led to chocolate, safety and ...

No! I lurched to a halt just outside the kitchen. I certainly wasn't running *home*. It wasn't that and never would be.

But ohhh, it smelt *so* wonderful anyway! It was exactly what I needed most right then – and, unlike the previous night, I didn't even have to try to resist it. Letting out all of my held breath in a *whoosh*, I dropped my rich, burgundy silk skirts, pushed the door fully open and swept like a queen into a completely different world.

Scented steam billowed through the whitewashed kitchen and surrounded me like a full-body hug. This room was only half the size of the Chocolate Heart's kitchen, but the familiar rattle of roasting cocoa beans sounded from the big fireplace at one end, and two heated braziers stood against the walls, along with two long counters, a big black oven, a sink and, best of all, three beloved figures who turned to face me as I stepped inside.

'Look who's here!' Horst leaned back against the bare wall, holding a gold-enamelled cup I'd never seen before. His quiet smile lit up his face, more warming to my heart than any fire. 'We've been waiting for you to stop by.'

'Well, well, well. If it isn't the royal princess herself, come to visit the little people on her rounds.' Marina's mouth quirked into a smile she couldn't quite hide as she poured an enticingly creamy, chocolatey mixture into one of the pie moulds that sat on her counter. 'Isn't our kitchen a bit common for a fine lady like yourself, madam?'

'Oh no,' said Aventurine, who was grinding down a sugar loaf at the far counter. 'She can't be a princess.' As she met my gaze across the room, her fierce golden eyes crinkled with amusement. 'Just look at her head,' she told the others. 'No crown.'

'Ohh!' Laughing, I mince-walked across the room as quickly as my skirts would let me. 'I missed you all *so much!*'

'Oof!' Aventurine let out a grunt as I grabbed her from behind for a tight hug. 'Careful of the sugar!'

'As if you'd ever let it fall.' Rolling my eyes, I released her and turned round to inspect everything. 'But where are all of your cups?'

The walls of the kitchen back in the Chocolate Heart were always covered with bright, colourful porcelain cups, and I knew and loved every one of them.

'Nowhere to put them.' Sighing, Marina waved at the bare white walls. 'They've stuck all their own cutlery in what they're calling "the chocolate room" next door. Silly things, those so-called cups.' She shook her head. 'They barely hold a thimbleful of hot chocolate each. All the same ...' She reached over to hook a bright copper kettle off the closest stovetop. 'See what you think. I've been tweaking my recipe for the royals.'

'Here.' I'd barely noticed Horst disappearing through the connecting door, but now he returned with another lovely, fragile-looking gold-and-white cup in a silver holder. 'I'll see if I can find a chair for you to sit in while we chat, Silke.'

Yearning stabbed through me despite myself as I looked around at their expectant faces. It would be so easy just to settle in and –

No. I wasn't working for them any more.

'I can't,' I said regretfully. 'I have to get back to the princesses and the welcome banquet. I'm only here to order up the royals' chocolate ... oh, and to pass on a message, too. An important one.' I took a deep breath, bracing myself for what was coming.

Dragons were notoriously bad at listening to good advice. So if I didn't approach this in exactly the right way ...

'Hmmph,' said Marina. 'You can stay long enough to

try one of my new hot chocolates at least. You don't want me sending something rotten to the royal visitors, do you?' She raised her eyebrows at me as she frothed the brass kettle of hot chocolate, rubbing the long wooden molinet briskly between her big, calloused palms. 'Besides, you look as if you need it. Haven't they bothered to find you a bed anywhere in this big palace? You look as if you haven't slept in a week.'

I shrugged uncomfortably, swallowing the yawn that wanted to rise up and split my head at the reminder. 'I've been busy,' I told her. 'I haven't had time to sleep.'

'Huh.' Marina's grunt reeked of scepticism as she poured out the steaming chocolate from the kettle.

She pushed the cup into my hands, and warmth shot up my arms. The scent of sweet, rich chocolate rose up through the air, dizzyingly delicious.

'Well ...' I took a deep breath and almost moaned with longing. 'Maybe I could stay just for a moment?'

'Of course you can.' Marina gave me a stern look as I lifted the cup to my lips, and Horst gently nudged a chair into place behind me. 'I expect you to finish every drop before you go, young lady. You can tell your *new* employers that you were busy giving us all sorts of irritating instructions. I take it the fairies have arrived and want some chocolate?'

'Mmm.' I closed my eyes in bliss as I sank down on to the chair and swallowed a long, luscious sip of liquid chocolate.

I had no idea what Marina had done to the recipe, but

the usual flare of heat had been toned down somehow, replaced by an extra roundness to the taste, as if a whole new layer had been added to the chocolate's story.

'This is *amazing*.'

'It would be even better if you'd kept all the usual chilli in it,' Aventurine said, still bent over the sugar loaf. 'I don't see why you had to take any out just because you were adding the other ingredients.'

Marina shook her head as she opened the oven door. 'For all we know, those fairies might never have tasted any spices from abroad, since they've been lurking under-ground for over a century.' She slid the last of the pies into the oven and stood up, closing the oven door with a firm *thunk*. 'Believe it or not, girl, not everyone likes the taste of flame as much as a dragon!'

Aha. I lowered my cup as nerves raced up my spine. 'That's what I was sent here to talk about.'

'What?' Marina twisted around to stare at me in open horror. 'Are you telling me those royals want to muck about with my recipes?'

'Marina ...' Horst winced, stepping forward.

Aventurine let out a low, warning growl, her eyes narrowing into golden slits. 'If they think, just because they *supposedly* own a few paltry little crowns, they can stomp all over *our chocolate* –'

Marina shook her head at me, ignoring the others. 'Didn't you *tell* them –?'

'Oh, for heaven's sake. They're *not even trying* to touch your precious recipes!' I bellowed over everyone.

Argh. So much for diplomacy!

As the three of them fell silent, gaping at me in shock, I swallowed down a hasty swig of hot chocolate to force my mouth shut before it could get me into more trouble.

'Silke?' Horst said tentatively. 'Is everything all right?'

Was everything all right? What a ridiculous question!

It was *too much*, that was the problem – it was *all* too much. Those horrible golden lights that had stolen my parents; the fairies' poisoned-honey words and glowing skin; that necklace that had landed on my shoulder, full of glittering temptation; and, worst of all, that familiar green darkness I had spotted beyond the doors ...

Elfenwald had followed me to Drachenburg after six years of freedom. Now that I was in a safe place – just for a moment – my whole body wanted to curl up in a shivering, teeth-chattering ball and never walk back towards it ever again.

Maybe this was how my parents' friends had felt six years ago, when they'd fled. Maybe ...

No. I jerked upright, setting down my hot chocolate and clenching my teeth together.

I wasn't going to abandon my parents again, no matter how I felt – and I wasn't about to let those magic-leaking fairies hurt my best friend either.

'I'm fine,' I told Horst firmly, 'only tired. I'll go back in just a moment. But ...' I captured Aventurine's golden gaze and gave her my very firmest look, '*you* aren't going anywhere.'

She sputtered out a disbelieving laugh. 'What are you talking about?'

'My job,' I told her flatly. 'I was hired to work out what the fairies really want, remember? Well, I have a bad feeling that the answer is *dragons*.'

CHAPTER 11

Aventurine's mouth dropped open. Her golden eyes widened.

'Ha!' She let out a shout of delighted laughter. 'I don't think so.' Shaking her head, she looked down at her sugar loaf and went back to grinding as thoroughly as if she had nothing left to worry about.

Dragons! I gritted my teeth. 'I'm serious!'

'Did they say they want to attack Aventurine's family?' Horst asked, frowning.

'Oh no.' I shook my head impatiently. 'They're *claiming* they only want proof we aren't lying about our alliance, so they can be sure that we're trustworthy trading partners.' I winced, thinking about my brilliant little handbill and the trouble it had brought me. 'They really, *really* care about the truth, apparently.'

And really, I did *mostly* tell the truth in almost every single circumstance. But was it so bad to twist it into a slightly better story every now and then?

'So they say.' Aventurine snorted. 'My grandfather says fairies will never tell a flat-out lie, but they're still the tricksiest, most untrustworthy creatures he's ever had cause to eat. Even worse than humans, if you can believe it!'

'Ah ... hmm.' I took that in for a long moment. 'Well, since you don't actually eat humans any more –'

'Oh, we never *wanted* to eat fairies in the first place.' Aventurine shrugged, looking perfectly untroubled. 'We never went after them – why would we want to? – but they kept coming after us for their own nonsense reasons, until they finally made everyone happy by going underground for good. Grandfather says eating them was the only way to stop them whenever they used to attack one of our nests. But he said they tasted absolutely *terrible*.'

'Huh.' Well, *that* was definitely not a story to be repeated near our visitors! But still ... 'Trust me,' I told her. 'Whatever they're after, it definitely involves your family. The crown princess knows it, too. That's why she sent me down here to warn you.'

'About what? A few fairies?' Aventurine shook her head, chuckling. 'Trust *me*. I don't have anything to worry about from them.'

'But if they find out what you really are –'

'I'm a *dragon*,' she said patiently. 'We *eat* fairies when they bother us. So –'

'You don't know them!' I was panting as I glared at her, green darkness creeping back into the corners of my vision. 'Oh, I know you've heard stories, but you have *no idea* how dangerous they can truly be. If you think for *one moment* that I'll let them take you, too, after everything –'

'"Too?"' A different voice cut me off. 'I thought you'd never met them before.' Marina's thick black eyebrows drew down over her frowning, dark gaze. 'Who else did they take from you, Silke?' she asked quietly.

I moistened my lips, my gaze caught in hers. For a moment, the whole story balanced on the tip of my tongue, just waiting to finally tumble out into the open for the first time in six long years of silence ...

But if I stopped holding it locked inside me, all of my old tears would come tumbling out along with it. I had been holding those tears back for *so* long now, ever since I'd first reached Drachenburg. I'd buried that story as deep as I could so that I could start again as a heroine, *not* a victim of *anyone*.

I was *supposed* to be blending in today. I had to smile and curtsey to the fairies and act as if I were utterly thrilled by their visit. If I let myself collapse now just because I felt safe, I would be a tear-stained mess for the rest of the day. I couldn't let that happen.

And more importantly, I *wouldn't* – because I knew exactly what my friends were like. They would insist on trying to help me if they couldn't manage to stop me. And then they would walk themselves straight into danger, arguing loudly all the way about how to do it.

I couldn't risk losing them, too.

'Nobody', I said firmly, and gulped the rest of my hot chocolate down in a rush as I stood, my rich silk skirts and thick petticoats billowing about me. 'But you were right about what you said last time, Marina: they're dangerous. So *keep Aventurine down here!*'

'I will *not* –!' Aventurine began in an outraged growl.

I swept magnificently to the door. 'Roar all you like', I carolled back. 'I don't mind! But the royals want chocolate served in the crown princess's private parlour after the banquet, so I'll send a maid down to tell you when it's time. Then she can do all the extra waitressing while you stay here and work on that sugar loaf.'

'I *won't* –!'

But I had no time to find out what Aventurine thought she wouldn't do. I slammed the door shut behind me and headed for the narrow servants' stairway with renewed purpose.

I was filled with hot chocolate. I was a heroine. I could do anything.

It was time to start seriously spying on the fairies.

Luckily, spy work turned out to be delicious.

The food that had been delivered to Sofia's apartments over the last few days had been better than anything I'd ever tasted that wasn't chocolate. But it was *nothing* compared to the feast spread out now to impress the fairy visitors.

Long, winding cabbage noodles had been mixed with

eggs and cheese and sculpted into artistic mountains and palaces that lined the six long tables until our greedy knives hacked into them. Moist, delectable chicken breasts exhaled luscious scents of baked cinnamon and raisins. Apple and pork dumplings, each one bigger than my fist, luxuriated in a savoury stew I could have dived into head first. Two roasted boars lay in proprietary splendour across every single table, with fresh, glistening red apples propped temptingly in their mouths.

I could have gorged myself for days. For *weeks*. For months, even! I still wouldn't have finished it all.

The entire riverbank community could have been fed all winter long and never gone hungry again.

I piled my plate as high as any of the real mountains outside Drachenburg and dug in with enthusiasm while I interrogated the fairy on my left ... who was only too ready to talk.

'Oh *no*,' she said with deep distaste as she eyed the mound of rich, cheesy cabbage noodles I'd just heaped beside my cinnamon-scented chicken. 'No, we certainly don't eat *that* in our home.' Her thin, glowing nostrils curled. 'We wouldn't dream of it.'

Countess von Silberstein was one of the oldest of the fairy queen's ladies-in-waiting, with ice-white strands glimmering amidst her upswept dark hair. But for all that she looked as elegant and terrifyingly magical as her rulers, five minutes of conversation were enough for me to realise who she *really* reminded me of: grumpy Frieda from the riverbank, for whom nothing was ever good enough.

I knew exactly how to talk to her.

'It must be awfully difficult for you,' I said sympathetically. 'Having to come all this way and eat such different food from what you're used to ...' Giving her my biggest, most soulful eyes, I popped a spoonful of apple dumpling into my mouth.

Oh, heaven! I stifled a moan with effort.

How could *anyone* complain about this meal?

'It *is* difficult!' She nodded vigorously, leaning forward. 'If you could only imagine the delights *we* are accustomed to enjoying underground – the exquisite refinement of the flavours – the delicacy of the ingredients the goblins gather for our pleasure –'

'Goblins?' I had to clap one hand over my mouth to keep from spraying my whole mouthful of dumpling on to the table. 'I mean –' I swallowed hastily – 'you have *goblins* down there, too?'

'Oh yes.' She waved one hand dismissively, her gaze sliding away from mine as she glanced at something past my shoulder. 'They are perfectly safe, you know, once you've set them the right bargain.'

'Oh, really?' This was my moment. I forced my voice to sound innocently curious. 'Who else is down there with you? Do you keep any humans there as household servants?'

'*Humans?*' Blinking, she glanced back at me, then let out a high, ringing peal of laughter. 'You think we would trust non-magical *humans* to look after us?'

The fairy queen cut off her own conversation, further

down the table, to call across, 'Good lord, Silberstein, I haven't heard you giggle so inanely for a quarter of a century, at least! What in the world is going on over there?'

'I do beg your pardon, Your Majesty.' The countess put one pale, glowing hand to her mouth. 'This young lady asked me if we kept humans as our household servants.'

'Ah.' Queen Clothilde gave the table at large a glittering smile. 'As yet, we have never found such a use for them. But perhaps, if these negotiations go as well as we all hope ...' She shrugged gently.

The way that her voice intentionally drifted off, and then she turned away, was an unmistakeable royal signal. The subject must now politely be dropped. I'd learned the rules of court life over the last week, and I recognised my cue even as it grated against my skin.

I couldn't ask any more questions now. If I did, I'd be hinting that I didn't trust the fairy queen's own statement – a direct insult to a royal from a mere underling.

So I closed my mouth obediently as she turned back to her own companions ...

But the questions in my head wouldn't stop itching at me, no matter how hard I tried to focus on the food that had seemed so tantalising only a few minutes earlier. Lowering my hands under the table, I twisted my fingers together, fighting for self-control.

A lady-in-waiting doesn't question her superiors.

A lady-in-waiting ...

How could I simply *let the subject drop*? I'd spent the last six years trying to answer that question! The truth was so close now, I could almost *feel* it hovering in the air above the lavish banqueting table.

If I could only keep the queen herself from hearing me …

I leaned closer to Countess von Silberstein, dropping my voice to a whisper. 'Aren't there *any* humans down there, though? All those travellers who've crossed the border over the last hundred years or so …'

'My goodness!' The fairy queen's voice snapped out, silencing every other conversation at the table as she glared at me. 'You *are* a curious creature, aren't you? Is it customary, in above-ground courts, for ladies-in-waiting to insult their visitors with such offensive questions?'

Oh, *mud*. She must have ears like a bat!

I lowered my gaze as my hands clenched under the table. Everyone was staring at me now. 'I beg your pardon, Your Majesty.'

'I should certainly think so! If –'

'My cousin is new to our court life, I'm afraid.' Princess Katrin flicked me a warning glance, but her tone was perfectly calm as she speared a cabbage noodle and twined it elegantly around her fork. 'She may be overly exuberant in her curiosity, but then, one does hear so many wild stories …'

'If one wants to banter about ridiculous *stories* –!' the fairy queen began.

Her husband coughed once, meaningfully, from his seat across the table. King Casimir did not speak or shake his head, but Queen Clothilde took a long breath as she watched him.

Then she smiled once again, letting out a high, artificial laugh. 'We can hardly remember every witless human traveller who's ever lost their way in our territory, can we?' She waved one hand in amused dismissal. 'We aren't executing the poor, ignorant creatures, if *that's* what those stories made you fear! So ...' She turned to our King Leopold on her other side. 'Tell me,' she said brightly, 'what is *your* favourite dish to eat out of all of these ... *interesting* offerings I see before me?'

Small talk took over the table again, and I let out my held breath in a *whoosh*. My heartbeat thrummed against my wrists and waves of warmth raced up and down my skin. I fought with all my might to stay still and keep my expression blank.

They're alive!

I could have leaped out of my chair and danced in front of everyone, humans and fairies alike.

Even Aventurine said the fairies never told a flat-out lie, for all that they twisted the truth into tricksy angles.

My parents really were alive!

I hadn't even realised, until that moment, just how much I'd dreaded the opposite possibility. The secret truth, although I'd never admitted it even to myself before, was that I'd been halfway certain of it. But now that I finally knew the real truth – *well*! If the fairies didn't keep them as household servants and didn't execute them either, all I had to do was find out what the fairies really *did* do with their human prisoners.

Oh, and one more thing: I had to work out how in the

world I was going to talk the crown princess into bargaining with the fairies for my parents' release ...

But all of that could be arranged, I was sure of it. *My parents were alive.* Now that I knew that, I could manage anything!

I dug into my meal, savouring every single, fresh, delicious bite ... until my neck suddenly prickled in warning, sending goosebumps skating down my spine.

Uh-oh. Someone was watching me from behind.

Still chewing, I twisted around in my seat as casually as I could. Red flashed past in the lower right-hand corner of my vision and disappeared before I could pick out what it had been ...

When I turned back to the table, I found the fairy king himself watching me with a thoughtful, considering expression.

Oops. I froze in mid-chew. Perhaps I hadn't done such a good job of *blending in* at this royal banquet after all.

Of course, it had been well worth breaking those ponderous rules of courtly manners – even if it had meant offending the visiting royals a bit – to find out that my parents hadn't been executed for trespassing, and yet ...

Swallowing down my last bite with an effort, I gave the fairy king my sunniest, most winning, *trust me!* smile.

He didn't smile back. He didn't look away either.

Oh, mud.

As his enigmatic gaze rested upon me again and again throughout the next two courses, my glorious food lost more and more of its flavour and a sick taste built up in the back of my mouth like a warning.

'Talk the fairies into trusting you,' the crown princess had instructed me.

My own secret quest might have made great strides at this banquet, but my official mission hadn't started well at *all*.

CHAPTER 12

I had never been so glad to finish a meal in my whole life. Thank goodness the royals were going off by themselves for their chocolate! I leaped to my feet the moment that the crown princess rose from the table, my chair legs scraping the floor behind me with a loud *squeeeeeak*.

The rest of the court followed suit in a noisy mass that almost drowned out Princess Katrin's next words.

'Thank you all for helping us to welcome our guests. We will be glad to see you again at tonight's scheduled entertainment. But in the meantime ...' Katrin nodded graciously at the fairy queen, 'I believe it's time to introduce the rulers of Elfenwald to a truly unique Drachenburg delight. Your Majesties ...' She held out one graceful brown hand. 'If you would care to withdraw with my family for a taste of our favourite local chocolate?'

'Hmmph,' muttered Countess von Silberstein beside me. 'We've certainly never eaten anything called *chocolate* back home! Isn't there any traditional food in this place?'

'It's *wonderful*,' I whispered back. 'And –' I couldn't help myself from adding it, even now – 'it's made by the best chocolatier in Drachenburg! She's probably the best in the whole world!'

'Hmmph,' the countess repeated sourly. But I thought I heard a trace of wistfulness in her tone as she watched her shining royals sweep towards the door in the crown princess's wake, leaving her and their other courtiers behind.

Sofia slid me a deeply satisfied look as she stalked after her sister, head held high, leaving *me* behind, too, on her way to that private royal conference. As usual, I knew exactly what the grumpy princess was thinking, because her face was like a public handbill, splashing out all of her thoughts for the world to see. She meant to catch me out with her sister by learning the fairies' secrets first herself.

I gave her my most serene, unworried smile in return … because I knew something that she didn't: I was going to get *so much* more out of the next hour than she was!

As Sofia stepped up to join the two bored-looking fairy princes – neither of whom bothered to make way for her – the crown princess suddenly turned around. 'Ah! Sofia, I've just had a charming idea. Do you think perhaps our ladies-in-waiting might show our other guests about the long gallery while we enjoy our chocolate?'

Aha. There it was. My beam intensified as Sofia's face fell.

She let out a sigh. 'How could I possibly say no?'

Princess Katrin gestured to the waiting footmen, who threw the great doors open. In a glittering, elegant swirl of colour, all seven royals swept from the room, with bobbing golden lights flaring all around them. It was such a breathtaking sight that the whole court watched it like a play.

Then the doors fell closed, leaving echoing silence behind.

Finally!

'Now, then', I said happily to the fairy countess beside me. 'Let us show you *everything*.'

Nearly thirty of us flooded out into the corridor once all the ladies- and gentlemen-in-waiting had been sorted out from the rest of the envious human courtiers.

With all of the royals safely gone, our party became far livelier within the next few minutes. The fairy king's gentlemen-in-waiting might have been hard-faced adult men, but among the young princes' gentlemen-in-waiting, some looked only a year or two older than me, and even the oldest of them could only have been seventeen or eighteen at the most.

Eerily glowing skin or not, they were still teenaged boys, which meant that three of them were jostling each other and sniggering within seconds; another one retrieved a glittering crystal toy from his robe and tossed it back and forth to himself as he walked; and two of the oldest ones slid into place beside Ulrike before we'd taken even five steps from the banqueting room.

Countess von Silberstein gave a huff of disapproval as she watched it all happen. 'Oh, *really!*' she began, starting forward.

But one of her friends among the queen's ladies-in-waiting pulled her back for some low-voiced gossip just in time, leaving me free to slide ahead on my own, aiming directly at the target I had chosen: the skinny boy with the crystal toy in his hands, walking apart from all the other gentlemen-in-waiting.

Perfect. I even knew his name, because I'd heard one of the princes call out to him earlier.

So I slipped into place beside him, grinning. 'Your name is Karl, isn't it? I'm Silke, and that's clever.' I pointed to the toy. 'Can I see it?'

Giving me a lopsided half-grin in return, Karl held his right hand up to show me. The crystal toy was shaped like a spinning top, but it never quite touched his skin as it twirled. Instead, it hovered half an inch above his glowing white palm, letting off an internal, sparkling light of its own, brighter than any diamond. The gasp that I let out as I looked at it was utterly sincere.

'Can I –?' I reached out one tentative finger.

'Sorry.' Karl smirked as the toy collapsed at my touch, falling down on to its side on his skin. 'Doesn't work for humans, I'm afraid. You need magic to play.'

'Ah,' I said knowledgeably. 'Like dragons, you mean.'

'Dragons?' He snorted, tossing the toy back into the

air as we rounded a corner of the corridor. 'If you knew anything about *dragons*, you'd know that they don't have any magic. They're even worse than you lot. At least some of your mages can do a bit – the way our toddlers would, really – but dragons are magic-killers, the worst of all.'

'Oh, really?' I raised one eyebrow, keeping my tone carefully casual. 'How do you know so much about them?' Only two of the fairies' golden lights had stayed with our big, chattering group, and they ranged one ahead and one behind the spread-out party – too far away, I hoped, to over-hear our conversation. Still, I kept my voice lowered as I asked, 'Haven't you lot been underground for over a century?'

He snorted, giving the toy an extra-fast spin. 'Why do you think we went underground in the first place?'

'*What?*' My feet stopped moving for a moment invol-untarily as I absorbed that.

Aventurine had claimed the fairies always came after the dragons, not the other way around – and dragons were *never* shy about admitting their aggressions. If they had chased the fairies underground, Aventurine would have bragged about that victory with pride.

But why would the fairies bother to flee from dragons who hadn't even attacked them in the first place?

I hurried to catch up with Karl. 'Wait a minute,' I said. 'Are you telling me –?'

But before I could finish my question, a hidden door swung open in the wall just beside me and nearly hit me in the face.

'Hey!' I skipped backwards. 'What – *oh*!'

It was Horst, stepping backwards into the corridor and carrying two large silver trays loaded high with chocolate. He winced as he looked around at the glittering crowd he'd stepped into; visibly relaxed as he spotted me; and then turned away in response to my warning glare, just as one of the fairy lights floated inquisitively towards him.

His eyes widened at that sight, but he'd served dragons and royals in the last few months, and he didn't allow himself to be sidetracked.

'Ahem.' He ducked his head politely in the closest courtier's direction. 'My lords and ladies, if you'll pardon me ...'

Of course. We were just by the winding staircase that led to the crown princess's private apartments. He must be on his way to make his delivery with the help of the maid I'd sent down earlier.

I let my gaze fall away from him with haughty aristocratic dismissal, drawing my silk skirts carefully out of reach and turning back to my companion ...

And then I heard a much-too-familiar snort.

No. I spun around, my breath catching in my throat with a sudden burst of panic. It *can't be* ...

But it was. Oh, *river mud*, it was!

Didn't dragons *ever* listen to common sense?

That maid I'd sent down to help serve the chocolate was nowhere to be seen. Instead, Aventurine swaggered into the corridor after Horst, balancing both of her own trays with careless strength. She didn't duck her head like a respectable servant; no, she turned from one startled noble to the next, staring each of them down with her feral golden gaze, until she finally turned to me with unmistakeable satisfaction.

Argh. Dragons were impossible!

I couldn't shout at her here. I wasn't even meant to know her.

But I knew exactly what she was thinking, with *absolutely typical* draconic arrogance, as she met my gaze now: '*See? I'm not afraid of any fairies!*'

My teeth ground together. My fingers curled into claws.

The boy beside me gave a startled jerk. 'Did you just *growl?*'

Ugh. 'I beg your pardon,' I muttered.

What was I *doing?* Unlike some people, I wasn't a feral animal. I had *self-control.* I had a *mission.*

I had a best friend I was going to *throttle* the very next time I got her alone!

Now she was striding away from me towards the fairy royals – with all of their schemes and their terrifying magic ...

Just like my parents had all those years ago.

As Aventurine and Horst walked through the door that led to the crown princess's stairway, the fairy sentinel that had been twirling towards them turned and fell back into place at the head of our party. It was only an advance scout, after all; there were plenty of others waiting ahead for my friends. The rest of those dazzling, sinister lights would all be gathered in the crown princess's apartments, forming a sparkling golden spiderweb around their fairy queen and king.

When my best friend swaggered into the room, they would fly straight at her, surround her and investigate her from top to bottom, and then, the moment they discovered what she really was –

'Um ... ?' Karl gave me a tentative prod.

All the rest of the courtiers had started moving again, bustling towards the long gallery ahead, with its delicious opportunities for gossip and relaxation.

It was exactly where I needed to be ... and when I glanced around, I found Countess von Silberstein and her gossipy friend standing close behind me, ready to poke my back with their long fingernails if I didn't move out of their way quickly enough.

'Aren't you coming?' Karl's feet shifted beneath his ankle-length robes. His pale eyebrows lowered with what looked dangerously like suspicion.

I gave him my warmest and most trustworthy smile. 'Of course I am!' I said.

What choice did I have? I had to find out more!

If the fairies really did blame the dragons for driving them underground in the first place, they must hate them even more than I had imagined ...

But my best friend – whose vulnerable scales weren't even halfway hardened yet – was walking straight into their arms while I just stood there.

'Well, young lady?' Countess von Silberstein snapped

behind me. 'Are you planning to stop lollygagging any time soon?'

My mission was waiting ahead of me.

My best friend was walking into danger without me.

I had been right: there really was no choice.

'Oh, I'm moving,' I told her firmly.

I spun around. Scooping up my long skirts with my left hand, I slammed my right hand into the wall beside me. The hidden door fell wide open, revealing the darkened servants' corridor beyond.

So much for blending in!

'What –?'

'I say –!'

As gasps and whispers broke out from every fairy and human courtier in my wake, I hurtled into the darkness and let the door fall closed behind me.

I had a dragon to rescue, whether she liked it or not.

CHAPTER 13

I could have run so much faster in my trousers, without a bothersome corset and petticoats to slow me down. But I didn't let my ladylike constrictions stop me. I hiked my heavy skirts up to my knees and let my long legs do their work even as my corset did its best to squeeze all the breath out of me. Thank goodness for those restless, sleepless nights; by now, I knew my way around the secret stairways and passageways of the palace almost as well as I'd known the streets of my city.

I burst through the right door less than a minute later, panting, with a stitch in my side and my lungs burning. But I'd done it: I fell into the crown princess's warm, luxurious private parlour just in time to see the public door start to crack open on my left.

Phew! I'd got there first ...

... And the entire roomful of powerful, scheming royals had just gone silent with shock at my arrival.

Oops. I hastily dropped my skirts to the ground.

Three plush golden couches had been drawn around the fireplace, and every one of the royals sitting atop those lovely couches – fairy and human alike – was turned towards me now, gaping in open horror ... including my own royal employer, who I'd promised to impress in my disguise as a proper lady-in-waiting. Only the ominous ticking of the grandfather clock in the corner broke the appalled silence.

I had navigated those narrow passageways just as cleverly as I'd ever cut through the alleyways of Drachenburg, yet in the process, not only had I failed to respect the royals' request for privacy, but I'd used a *servants'* path to do it – something no true aristocrat would ever do.

Time to think up a really good story, Silke.

'Your Majesties.' I swept my deepest and most perfectly polished curtsey to the two royal families.

Something popped in the fireplace.

The crown princess's mouth snapped shut.

Her father scowled in obvious confusion beside her.

I smiled hopefully as I straightened ... and kept smiling even as golden lights swirled and spun towards me from all across the room.

'I do beg Your Majesties' pardon,' I said sweetly. In the corner of my eyes, I glimpsed Horst stepping through the public doorway, with Aventurine at his heels, but none of the fairy sentinels bothered with them; they were too busy swarming towards me in a buzzing cloud of suspicion.

Who could blame them? No real lady-in-waiting would ever act this way. Even I knew that.

My smile felt frozen and artificial on my face, but I forced myself to keep talking as the sinister lights closed in around me, blocking the royals from my view and filling my vision with sparkling, dangerous gold.

'I know it's terribly impertinent of me to burst in like this, but I couldn't resist. I saw all of that delicious chocolate being brought here, and I was *so* excited, I simply had to beg a boon from my royal cousins. *May* I please serve the chocolate to our honoured visitors? It seems so wrong for them to be served by mere ...' A golden light zoomed much too close to my face and hovered blindingly between my eyes. '... Mere shopworkers', I finished weakly.

There was a muffled sound from the doorway.

Shut up, Aventurine. Shut up, shut up, shut up!

I breathed deeply, closing my eyes as the golden lights pressed against me from all sides.

Could they read minds? I didn't think so.

I hoped they couldn't.

I thought as hard as I could, just in case: *I'm a lady-in-waiting. Only a lady-in-waiting. Really!*

I was the worst spy ever. The crown princess might never forgive me for making such a spectacle of myself on my first day of *blending in*.

But if the fairy sentinels were swarming me, they weren't swarming my best friend – and I wasn't letting them steal anyone else I loved away from me.

'Isn't this the same chit who was pestering us with such offensive questions at the banquet?' The fairy queen's sharp voice was unmistakeable.

'My newest lady-in-waiting.' And *that* was Sofia, letting out a sigh that sounded worryingly satisfied. 'We took her in as a favour because she's distant family, but I'm afraid she hasn't acquired any real polish yet.'

Ouch! That injustice stung. I had spent *all week* being polished and learning perfect court manners every bit as good as Sofia's own.

But it was hard to argue about my sophistication now as I stood, still struggling for breath, in front of the wide-open servants' door, while the golden lights that had stolen my parents swirled around me from top to bottom.

As I held myself frozen still, they brushed closer and closer against my cheeks and ears and hair, letting out a high-pitched humming noise that shivered against my bones until I had to dig my fingernails into my palms just to keep myself from lashing out at them in horror. *Don't scream, don't scream, don't scream …*

'I can send her back to my apartments for the remainder of your visit, if you'd prefer,' Sofia offered sweetly.

That little sneak! Outrage punctured my bubble of terror. My mouth dropped open.

'I'm certain that will *not* be necessary.' The crown

princess's voice cut like steel through the charged air. 'However, our impetuous young cousin does have a point. Perhaps our guests do deserve a more personal welcome. In fact ...' She paused. 'Sofia, why don't *you* serve our esteemed visitors?'

Oh, lord. I sucked in a breath.

I really was in trouble now. I didn't need to see Sofia's face to know how she would react to that command.

Princesses never served *anyone.*

But as the mass of golden lights around me began to thin, flocking back to their different outposts throughout the room, Sofia rose reluctantly to her feet and trudged, scowling, to where Horst and Aventurine waited by the doorway.

The older fairy prince sniggered and elbowed his younger brother. The younger one smirked.

Every gaze in the room was fixed on the outlandish spectacle of a princess acting as a parlourmaid ... which meant that not a single fairy royal showed a fraction of interest in the mere chocolatier's apprentice whose job Princess Sofia was about to perform.

Perfect.

Sofia stuck out her jaw at a stubborn angle as she pulled the first heavy tray out of Aventurine's arms ... and then she staggered, cups clinking, under its weight.

I could have told her how heavy those trays were!

But I felt some reluctant admiration as the grumpy princess squared her shoulders and rebalanced the tray with a visible effort. For better or for worse, Sofia never gave up on anything. As soon as she had that first tray in place, she jerked her chin at Aventurine, who passed her the next one with ease.

With her face squeezed tight in concentration, the younger princess shuffled at a snail's pace all the way back to the elegant table that had been placed in the middle of the semicircle of couches.

Cups shivered and rocked dangerously on their plates until –

Phew. I let out my held breath as she placed the second tray on the table. *Nothing broken!*

'There.' She nodded jerkily to Horst, who set down the next two trays. 'You can go.'

He nodded and backed away in silence. *Wise man.*

My breath caught in my chest as I glimpsed the fury burning in Sofia's eyes. For now, though, it wasn't aimed at me.

She lifted the first of the tall silver chocolate pots. 'Hot chocolate, Katrin?' Her voice was sickly sweet.

'Why, thank you, sister.' The crown princess smiled back at her.

The door closed behind my friends at the other side of the room, and my shoulders finally began to relax.

Out of danger. At least, Aventurine was.

As for me ...

'You may leave us, Silke,' the crown princess said as her sister poured steaming, dark hot chocolate into a delicate porcelain cup. 'Unless you have any more burning impositions that *must* interrupt our private conference?'

My shoulders tightened all over again as the younger fairy prince let out a snort of laughter.

Keeping my face expressionless, I lowered myself into a submissive curtsey. 'No, Your Highness. Thank you, Your Highness.'

'Hmm.' Her gaze raked over me. 'We'll discuss this further tonight after the theatrical performance.'

'Oh yes, Your Highness,' I agreed with deep relief.

That would work *perfectly*. I could safely report all of my findings to her while everyone else imagined she was merely giving me a royal dressing-down. If I could only come up with enough information by then to persuade her to forgive me ...

'Indeed,' drawled the fairy king. 'I believe my wife and I would quite like a word or two with this unusual ... *Silke* ... as well.'

Oh, river mud!

I glanced up involuntarily and found him watching me with a horribly enigmatic expression.

The fairy queen's expression wasn't enigmatic at all. It was pinched tight with suspicion.

It certainly wouldn't take a genius to realise that a lady-in-waiting who'd only recently arrived at court shouldn't know her way around the servants' passageways, much less burst through royal walls when they thought they were having a private conference. And when she asked suspicious questions about Elfenwald secrets ...

I wondered what they did to spies in the fairy court.

But I was still a lady-in-waiting as well as a spy, so

I murmured, 'I would be honoured, of course, Your Majesties' as I backed towards the servants' door, panic pounding through me.

I had to get away from this room full of danger. I had to …

'Ahem.' The crown princess cleared her throat, stopping me in my tracks. She raised her eyebrows pointedly.

Oops.

Remember which world you're moving in, Silke!

Turning as smoothly as I could, I glided with the exquisite grace of an aristocratic lady towards the public door – my *only* possible exit, as a lady-in-waiting.

But I didn't go alone.

Two golden fairy sentinels flew across the room to join me as I mince-walked towards the door. Buzzing loudly, they bobbed up and down in front of my face as if to make certain I knew that they'd taken my measure. Then they settled into place like prison guards, one on either side of my shoulders.

Oh, perfect. The fairy royals must have assigned me an escort. I really had caught their interest now, hadn't I?

My teeth gritted behind my smile as I held my head high and swept out through the door.

My spying mission had just become ten times harder.

CHAPTER 14

The moment I stepped into the long gallery five minutes later, the room went silent.

Then the whispers began.

Conversations broke off in every group I passed. Heads jerked around to stare at me. Voices dropped into malicious, gossiping tones.

My skin tingled under the pressure of all those avid stares.

When I finally spotted Karl standing with a group of other fairy courtiers, he took one look at me, winced and then turned his back.

Ouch! I teetered to an abrupt halt at the snub, almost tripping over my long skirts. So much for finding out any more useful details from him!

I stood alone in the centre of the long room, with my two golden escorts humming ominously by my sides and at least a dozen sneering aristocratic gazes inspecting every angle of my flushing face.

It was my worst nightmare come to life.

Ever since that horrible night on the riverbank when I'd watched angry townspeople burn down our tents, I had sworn that – no matter what it took – I would *never* let anyone look at me and see a dangerous outsider again.

Standing there, I could almost smell those flames in the air once more.

The chocolate kitchen downstairs, warm and cosy and safe, called up to me with an almost audible siren song. The winding streets outside the palace waited, familiar and beloved, for me to run down them to freedom.

I squared my shoulders before they could hunch, and I turned around in a slow circle to meet the gaze of every single sneering courtier – because this time, I wasn't going to give into my terror.

So I couldn't *blend into* this glittering crowd? Then I would throw myself with all of my might into *standing out*, no matter how uncomfortable and exposed that might make me feel.

I would not give up on my parents again!

Beaming furiously, I picked up my skirts and swept across the polished wooden floor to the closest group of fairy ladies-in-waiting. 'My *goodness!*' I carolled as I forced my way into their circle, ignoring their raised eyebrows and the way they tugged their skirts away as if I might taint them by getting too close. 'Do you know *what* our rulers are eating in the crown princess's private parlour? I could hardly believe it when I saw it with my own eyes!'

Well. They weren't about to give up the opportunity of hearing those privileged details, even from a wild, unmannerly girl like me.

And when I managed to pull in Anja and Lena from their own groups a few minutes later, it was only too easy to say, 'Actually, that reminds me of a story ...'

'A story?' Lena's eyes brightened. She clapped her hands together. 'Oh, Silke tells the best stories!'

'She really does', Anja agreed, so enthusiastically that two nearby fairy gentlemen-in-waiting wandered over to join our crowd.

The fairy sentinels on either side of me pressed closer and closer, until they were vibrating against my neck, sending hot-and-cold shivers racing up and down my skin.

'*Stories?*' Countess von Silberstein huffed sceptically. 'What nonsense!'

What nonsense indeed. As the glowing fairies and their sentinels closed in around me, bringing up the very worst memories of my life, the blood pounded harder and harder in my ears, until every clear thought in my head was obscured by a fog of pure panic. For once, there was no chance at all that I might think up something dazzling and new for their entertainment.

But there had never been a better moment to remember who had taught me how to tell stories in the first place.

Even the snobby countess listened intently as I launched into one of my mother's very best tales. It was full of perilous adventures and magic – my favourite kind – with a girl who braved ice giants and a wicked king to set her true love free from a music mage's spell.

It had been so long since I'd heard that story. I'd never told it to anyone in my life. It was *mine*. It had always felt too precious to be shared. But as I spoke the familiar words for the first time in years and sank back into the adventure, I found myself relaxing just like the crowd around me, all of us caught up together in its spell.

For one enchanted moment, I could almost *feel* my mother's presence surrounding me; the warmth of her words in my mouth pouring through me as if I were lying tucked up in her arms once again, listening to her stories on my way to sleep.

I'd always felt so certain, back then, that there *would* be a happy ending for all of those characters – and for me ...

By the time I'd finished the story, there was a whole crowd of fairy courtiers gathered around, joining in with their own ideas and reactions to the tale.

'If I'd faced that ice giant ...'

'All she needed was to cast it into sleep, or –'

'No, she should have set a proper bargain to control it! If –'

'Do ice giants really bargain?' Karl frowned thoughtfully.

'*Everyone* bargains', said the youngest of the fairy queen's ladies-in-waiting, flicking her fan at him with icy disdain. 'Except for humans and dragons, of course.'

Of course? I blinked at that, remembering a dozen or so bargains I'd made over the last month alone. But I didn't have time to seize upon that point – not when there was such a perfect conversational pathway for me to leap down instead.

'Well', I said with relish, 'if you want a story about *dragons* ... !'

But before I could launch properly into my next tale, the doors at the far end of the gallery flew open.

Sofia stalked into the room, followed by the two fairy princes. Prince Franz and Prince Ludolph sauntered together a few lazy steps behind my grumpy princess, but from the maliciously amused curls of their lips and the enraged look on Sofia's flushed brown face, I would wager anything that they hadn't spent the journey in silence.

They may have been sent off to socialise while the adults hammered out the real business but, apparently, diplomacy was *not* going well among the younger members of the royal families.

Sofia took one sweeping look around the gallery. Her gaze fixed on the large group that had gathered around me. Her brows lowered ominously. 'Silke!' Her voice rang out through the room. 'I need you.'

Argh! My teeth ground together. Sofia didn't need anything from me – she just didn't want me succeeding in any spy work ahead of her.

Smiling over my clenched teeth, I ducked a brief curtsey to the remaining fairy courtiers. 'Perhaps I can tell that story later?'

I moved as swiftly as I could, but Sofia was tapping one finger impatiently against her side as I joined her only a moment later.

'Finally,' she muttered.

'Your Highness.' I curtseyed deeply, conscious of the two fairy princes watching us both with sardonic looks, as if we were exotic animals in a menagerie performing for their amusement. 'May I be of some assistance?'

She gave me a thin smile, her eyes glittering. 'Oh, I've come up with the perfect use for you.'

Uh-oh. What was she planning?

According to her sister's orders, I had to be allowed here to do my work. But if Sofia could think up any clever ways to stop me from getting it done without actually banishing me from the room ...

'You can keep me company,' she said firmly. 'I want you by my side from now on. Do you understand?'

'Perfectly,' I said in my sweetest tone.

The younger princess had just won this round of our personal battle.

As I glided across the gallery in Sofia's wake, I smiled and I curtseyed, but – because I was waiting on her – I kept my lips tightly sealed. My chest burned with the frustration of so many bottled words, but I didn't dare damage my disguise any further.

A lady-in-waiting *never* spoke over her royal mistress or tried to direct royal conversations – not even when her princess was making an *utter hash* out of everything we needed from our fairy visitors!

'Any problems at home?' Sofia was a five-foot battering ram of interrogation as she waved one small brown hand impatiently at the fairy queen's most elegant lady-in-waiting. 'Territorial disputes? Trade issues? Anything you've been particularly hoping for help with on this visit?'

The lady-in-waiting – who was at least forty years old, statuesque and full of self-importance – smiled disdainfully as she curtseyed. 'Your Highness cannot possibly imagine,' she murmured, 'that Elfenwald would require any human help in our own kingdom.'

Oh no? My eyes narrowed at her answer.

These fairies found the idea of relying on humans to be truly laughable, didn't they? I remembered Countess von Silberstein's helpless giggles at the banquet. What was it, exactly, that made us so useless in their eyes? Was it only our lack of magic, or something more?

More importantly: if we really *were* so worthless to them, why would they even bother to capture any human trespassers?

There were so many questions waiting to be asked! Off the top of my head, I could think of at least five different responses that might draw out that lady-in-waiting to say a great deal more about Elfenwald and its secrets.

But of course I couldn't speak … and Sofia's face screwed up as if she'd bitten into a lemon. 'You needn't act as if we were completely useless!' she snapped. '*Your rulers* were the ones who begged my sister for this visit, you know! And if you think for even one moment –'

'Ahem!' I coughed desperately into my hand as every fairy courtier around us stared at her in mounting outrage. Even the human courtiers were cringing in dismay.

Sofia shot me a dismissive glare. 'Oh, *do* stop coughing and come along, Silke.' Tilting her chin, she swept away from the simmering lady-in-waiting. 'Clearly, there is nothing more of interest for us here!'

Chilli hot chocolate. Almond fancies. Chocolate creams ... In desperation, I took a moment to stand still and recite the Chocolate Heart's menu in my head. It was the only way I could keep myself from screaming out loud.

Didn't she have *any idea* how important this mission really was?

'Silke!' Her voice snapped through the air.

I breathed deeply, letting the air slowly out through my nose.

Of course the princess didn't know how important this was. How could she? *She* had everything she needed already. All that Sofia wanted was to impress her sister, and she wouldn't lose anything if she failed.

I was the only one who truly needed this to work ...

But I had a horrible feeling that I was running out of time.

CHAPTER 15

'Silke.' The crown princess stopped me from following her sister that evening as the music room emptied.

The famous puppet theatre's slapstick performance was long finished. The elegant string quartet had played their final chords, and the fifth and last round of after-supper drinks and snacks had been whisked away by servants.

The fairy queen had even summoned all of her sentinels back to her side. Now they surrounded her tall figure in a whirl of lights, like golden flies returned to a sparkling spiderweb.

My own two terrifying sentinel lights had let out a high-pitched whine that grated against my ears, hovering beside me for a long moment after their mistress first held out her arms in summons ... but even they had peeled away from me in the end to rejoin the rest of their comrades, giving up their spy work for the evening.

The night sky stretched like a thick, black velvet cloth outside the broad glass windows of the music room, and every human and fairy courtier streamed towards the doorway, heading for their beds ...

Except for me.

'A word in private, if you please.' Princess Katrin's tone left no room for disagreement.

Anja and Lena winced with sympathy as I fell back from their bustling group. Ulrike gave a disapproving sniff.

Muffled snorts came from other nearby courtiers, and my spine tightened an extra notch.

Everyone knew by now that the crown princess had promised me a royal lecture tonight.

But Sofia stalked out of the room ahead of me without any noticeable satisfaction on her face ... because she was the only other person who knew what else was about to happen: I was going to give her sister my first real spy report.

I only wished that I had something better to offer in it.

Still, I knew better than to start with an admission of weakness. So the moment that the door to the crown princess's private library closed behind us ten minutes later, I gave her my most enthusiastic smile and rubbed my hands together.

'Well!' I began. 'If you ask me –'

'What in the world have you been thinking?' Princess Katrin wheeled around to glare at me. Padded green velvet wing chairs stood ready by the magnificent marble fireplace, but she ignored them, standing ramrod straight. 'Did you or did you not promise me that you would pass for a plausible member of my court?'

My heartbeat was suddenly pulsing hard against my throat. I backed up a step before I could stop myself. 'Your Highness, if I may take just a moment to explain –'

'Do you really imagine you can play that game with me?' The disdain in her voice was scalding. 'You promised to discreetly persuade my visitors into trusting you. Instead, you clowned about all day long as if you were playing at some lark with your little friends from the third district! If you think you can win *me* around with a bit of fast-talking and a smile –'

'No! Your Highness, I never thought ...' I swallowed, but I couldn't pull any moisture into my parched throat. My voice cracked horribly on my next words. 'This isn't a game. Not for me.'

'Then perhaps you're just naturally incompetent.' She let out a gusting sigh. 'You couldn't even manage to keep your dragon friend out of sight, could you? I thought at least *she* would have listened to you. The fairies certainly never will after today.'

'Please!' I took a quick step forward. 'I know I haven't blended in, but –'

Katrin's icy gaze halted me in my tracks. 'First,' she said, 'you made both Casimir and Clothilde suspicious with your impolitic questions at the banquet – none of which had *anything* to do with the task I'd set you! Then you behaved like a buffoon playing hide-and-seek in the midst of our royal visit – and worse still, a buffoon who *didn't know her own rank.* Would you say that bursting in through a servants' doorway made your disguise more convincing to any of our guests?'

'No, Your Highness.' I winced. 'But I didn't have a choice. You see –'

'And *then*,' she continued inexorably, 'instead of keeping your head down in the aftermath to let everybody else forget your antics, you attracted the attention of every member of the fairy court by lowering yourself to the status of an *entertainer.* As if any true aristocrat would *ever* play the part of a court jester!'

What? My mouth dropped open. Shock mingled with sudden fury in my belly, boiling up towards my throat like bile.

That had been *my mother's story* that I'd told the fairies! I'd made the sacrifice of sharing something important – something truly dear to me – with those snobby courtiers for the sake of succeeding in her mission. And she –

Stop.

I took a deep breath, forcing down my emotions.

My mother needs me not to give up now.

'I was trying,' I said steadily, 'to draw them out. And it was *working*, too, until – mmm!' I cut myself off just in time as her eyebrows rose threateningly.

138

For one silent moment, our gazes held. Hers was full of an unmistakeable warning.

Of course Katrin had seen the way Sofia had kept me chained to her side all day. She knew as well as I did what had stopped me.

But I knew better, by now, than to complain about either sister to the other – and if I couldn't manage against the younger princess's hostility, then I couldn't hope to save my position here.

No excuses.

'Please,' I said instead, 'let me try again. I'm already finding out useful information for you! If you'll only give me one more chance ...'

'Oh, really.' Katrin turned away from me to gaze down into the fireplace. Shadows flickered across her face. 'Tell me exactly what valuable secrets you've learned for me today.'

I drew myself up like a soldier on inspection. 'I can tell you exactly what the fairies are here for. *Dragons.*'

The crown princess's reaction wasn't what I had hoped.

'*Dragons.*' She let out a crack of laughter, shaking her head to herself. For the first time since I'd met her, her straight shoulders sagged. 'After all that kerfuffle and nonsense with doors, *that's* all you have to tell me? That the fairies are here because of our recent treaty?'

'Well ...' I ran my tongue nervously over my upper lip. 'I thought –'

'Even an infant could have picked up on their fascination

with our allies', Princess Katrin said coolly. 'Added to the fact that they brought that foolish handbill of yours along with them, it hardly took much deduction to puzzle that much out.' Her upper lip curled. 'Please, Silke, do trust me to have *some* wits of my own. What I *would* be interested in hearing ...' She cocked her head as she studied me. 'Did you happen to find out, in all of your *unusual* efforts today, exactly what they have planned for our allies?'

'Not ... not exactly', I admitted. *Not at all.* 'But it really can't be anything good, because –'

'I thought not.' She sighed and turned away, silencing me with a wave of her hand. 'Never mind. It was an interesting experiment while it lasted. At least I needn't waste any more time wondering about your usefulness.'

Her tone firmed, turning businesslike. 'You may spend one more night here, so as not to cause suspicion among Sofia's other ladies-in-waiting. But I can promise you that after the events of today, *none* of them will be surprised to see you leave in the morning, as many other regrettable ladies-in-waiting have left before. Moreover, you'll receive a payment for your time that should be more than enough for you to forget everything you saw and experienced while you were here. So –'

'Wait!' Lights were flashing in front of my eyes. Dizziness swept over me until I staggered.

I *couldn't* fail. I couldn't leave! Not when I was so close to finding my parents.

'Please', I begged. 'I *have* found out something important, I swear. The dragons are the reason the fairies went underground in the first place! If you'll just give me one more day to find out exactly why, and what they're planning ... I'll give up my payment. I'll –'

'To what purpose?' Katrin pinned me with an icy glare. In her eyes, I saw the ruthless ruler who'd chosen the fate of her city over my best friend's life four months ago. 'There's no use in arguing,' she said. 'You may have picked up one intriguing titbit, but you certainly won't find any more. You should have known it was too late from the moment you attracted the fairies' interest. Even if you were the cleverest spy in the world, you'd never learn anything of value with two fairy sentinels marking your every move – and after the number of questions I've already been asked about you by our royal visitors, you can rest assured you *would* be followed by their spies for the rest of your time here.'

With a swish of her skirts, she settled down in the wing chair closest to the fireplace. The light from the flames mingled with the candlelight nearby to burnish her light brown skin and make her dark eyes glitter. She was by far the most beautiful person I'd ever seen in my life, and she was crushing every hope I'd ever had for my future.

'Goodbye, Silke,' said the crown princess. 'We thank you for your services, which will no longer be required. Enjoy your final sleep in the palace.'

'Your Highness,' I murmured through cold lips as I swept her my finest ever curtsey.

My final sleep ...

If she thought I was going to sleep now, she was mad!

As I glided like a lady through the corridors of the palace, I felt as if I were floating above my body, light with panic and too full of purpose to even feel the ground beneath me.

I had one final night to prove myself. I wasn't going to waste a single minute of it.

When I joined the other ladies-in-waiting in our room, I turned away all of their worried questions with a laugh.

When Anja asked me to tell them another story, I made a funny, apologetic face and told her that I was too tired at the moment, but that tomorrow I absolutely, definitely would ... even as the crown princess's words burned in my memory.

'As if any true aristocrat would ever play the part of a court jester!'

There was no time to be hurt, or even to worry that she might have been right. Instead, I stood calmly as our maid changed me into my borrowed nightgown, like a rich girl's porcelain doll being dressed.

I smiled sweetly at the other girls as I tucked myself under the bedclothes, and then, despite the impatience that burned through my muscles, I held myself still and silent as I waited for their nervous giggles and whispered speculation ('Do you think those fairies stay awake all night?' and 'Do you think they eat worms down underground?') to shift into rattling breaths and snores.

Finally, *finally*, nearly an hour later, I crept out of my bed in bare feet and tiptoed across the warm carpet, thankful all the way down to my bones for every illicit trip of exploration I'd made during the previous long nights.

This time, I knew exactly where I was going.

I padded, whisper soft, past Sofia's closed bedroom door with the ease of long practice. I slipped through the darkened outer salon without bumping into a single couch or wooden side table along the way. The hidden door in the salon wall opened like an old friend at the touch of my hand.

Silent as a shadow, I slid into the pitch-black corridor beyond. Then I let out a sigh of relief and strode forward, giddy and tingling with the exhilaration of *finally* taking over my own story.

I was a heroine, setting out alone against impossible odds.

I was the underdog on her way to unexpected but inevitable victory!

I was –

'Argh!'

I was suddenly tripping and crashing forward in the darkness, arms windmilling helplessly as I fell on to a warm, breathing lump on the floor ...

Because tonight, I wasn't alone after all.

Someone – or *something* – had been waiting for me.

CHAPTER 16

'Oof!' I landed hard on my elbows, half sprawled across that waiting figure.

It twisted hard underneath me, and I jerked, trying to jump back to safety ...

But the door was already swinging closed behind me. It shut me into the pitch-darkness of the servants' passageway as a low growl rumbled through the stale air and I scrabbled backwards.

What else had the fairies brought along with them?

'Couldn't you have knocked first?' Aventurine snarled.

'Ohhh!' I collapsed across her, limp with relief. My heart was still thrumming against my ribs as if I'd just sprinted across the entire first district. 'What are you *doing* here, you idiot?'

'What do you think?' Yawning, she pulled herself free. I heard the scuffling sounds of her pushing herself up into a sitting position. 'Looking after you, of course.'

'After *me*?' I shook my head in bafflement as I sat up, tucking my knees against my chest. 'You're the dragon, remember? *You're* the one all those fairies want to catch, not me.'

'Pah.' Her snort ruffled through the enclosed air. 'I told you, I'll eat any fairy who tries.'

'And I told *you* –!' No. I gritted my teeth against the furious response that wanted to spill out of me. I had too little time left to waste my breath. '*Anyway*,' I said, 'aren't you supposed to be sleeping in the chocolate kitchen while you're here?'

'The kitchen's fine,' Aventurine told me. 'Unlike you, it isn't going anywhere. But I knew you'd do something ridiculous like sneaking around at night with nobody to protect you.' She sighed with aggravating condescension. 'You may act like a dragon from time to time, but you don't actually have claws or teeth, you know.'

I bared my blunt teeth at her in the darkness. 'You think not?'

'Not real ones,' she said flatly. 'So someone has to look after you.'

It was too much. I started laughing. But as I tipped my head on to my knees, my laughter wobbled dangerously. I had to blink my stinging eyes again and again, gulping back everything that wanted to escape in the safety of darkness.

'What is it?' Aventurine sounded suspicious. 'What are you doing? It doesn't sound right.'

'It's just ...' I shrugged helplessly, drawing a deep breath to push down the last of the tears. 'Haven't you figured it out by now? No *one* looks after me. That's not how it works. I look after myself. Always.'

And I was good at it. At least, I used to be, before I'd dived in over my head, so stupidly, hopelessly over-confident that I could manage every new challenge at the palace ...

No. That was the victim of a story speaking, not a *heroine.* I wasn't going to admit defeat now!

I sprang to my feet, slapping my hands briskly together. 'So! I've got to get to work. But you can go back to sleep now that you know I'm fine, and –'

'I don't think so,' said Aventurine. The air of the narrow passageway shifted around me as she rose to her feet. Her warm arm brushed against mine. 'I'd like to see a real human spy at work.'

'But –'

'I know you won't mind,' she said coolly, 'since you've got everything so perfectly under control ... right?'

I'd been sacked by the crown princess.

I'd been marked out by the fairies.

I had less than six hours left to save my family and my future.

I swallowed a laugh before it could turn into outright hysteria.

'Right,' I told her. 'Perfectly.'

* * *

Unfortunately, dragons had no idea how to be stealthy.

'Shh!' I hissed five minutes later as Aventurine slammed yet another door behind her. We were on our way to the hidden passageways of the south-east wing, where the fairy visitors were housed, and the echoes of that slam made my whole body twitch. 'We don't want them to hear us coming!'

'*Pfft*,' Aventurine snorted. 'I told you, I'm not afraid of fairies.'

'*Grr!*' I let out a low, dragon-ish growl of my own as I rubbed my fingers hard over my hair. Exhaustion throbbed behind my temples. All those nearly sleepless nights in a row made it hard to remember how to be clever or diplomatic, or anything but tired and ... well, terrified.

I *couldn't* fail tonight. I just couldn't.

'Look,' I hissed, 'I know you're all about stomping and roaring and taking over territory, but that's not what human spies do. We need to sneak around *very quietly*, and try to see if we can pick up any secrets. So if you care *at all* about me and my family, you'll pretend that you're not a big, scary predator, just for the next half hour of your life. All right? Is that too much to ask?'

There was a long, pulsating moment of silence in the narrow corridor.

Then Aventurine said, 'What does your family have to do with this?'

Oh, *mud*. 'I'll tell you later,' I promised. 'But in the meantime, can't you please just trust me? Just for now?'

'Of course I trust you,' Aventurine said.

There was such obvious bafflement in her voice – bafflement that I'd ever question her trust – that I found my chest tightening unexpectedly, a sudden burst of warmth swelling irrepressibly within me.

'*Of course* I *trust you.*'

Who else in my life would ever say that? Dieter would have laughed – or worse, sighed – at the very idea of it. The crown princess, who should have understood me better, had refused to even listen to my explanations today ... and she'd called me a buffoon. I'd been trying so hard not to let those words sink through my skin.

I hadn't realised just how much I did need a friend tonight.

Reaching out in the darkness, I found Aventurine's arm – strong and muscled from all of her kitchen-work – and squeezed hard.

'What?' She laughed. 'Was that supposed to be a puny human attack?'

'No.' Smiling, I let go. 'I'm just glad that you're here with me. But you still have to *be quiet!*'

'Oh, fine.' She sighed heavily. 'But I'll only do it to make you happy, not because I'm afraid of any puny fairies.'

'Whatever.' I rolled my eyes. 'Now, take off your shoes, and let's keep going.'

But the warmth in my chest didn't dissipate as we slipped on soft, shoeless feet through the dark of the hidden corridors in the guest wing.

There were, officially, no servants' corridors in this

part of the palace: that was what all the royal visitors were told. The regular servants' corridors came to a halt at a solid wall before the guest wing, as far as any newcomer could tell, giving a false impression of security. If you knew where to go, though – and which hidden panels to press – there were just as many ways to travel unnoticed behind the guest rooms as behind any others in this palace ... at least, as long as you didn't carry any lights with you to give yourself away.

Aventurine's eyesight was sharper than a regular human's, even in her two-legged form, and I'd learned these corridors by feel, but this time I didn't need to rely on my memory. Narrow streams of light pierced the darkness at odd angles tonight: candlelight from the fairies' rooms, escaping through the peepholes that had been hidden in their walls.

This palace was designed to steal secrets.

Unfortunately, no matter how many peepholes I stood at, no secrets seemed waiting to be found – only people, glowing strangely but still surprisingly similar to all the humans that I had left behind me. Not a single one of them was loudly hatching plans or helpfully discussing what they did with trespassers like my parents. Instead, each new conversation I overheard was filled with exactly the same kind of anxious speculation in reverse that I'd over-heard in my own shared bedroom.

'... Well, I've heard that whenever people disagree with the crown princess, she has them fed to her pet dragons!'

'... That's why you don't see any of our kind in the

court! They're taken prisoner the moment the dragons spot them coming, and then if they won't give away the secrets of *our* court, the king and crown princess let the dragons tear them to bits in the public square to frighten their people into submission.'

'... They probably only agreed to that treaty in the first place so they could attack Elfenwald together. You know every kingdom on this continent wants to steal our silver ...'

At the phrase 'pet dragons', I'd slammed one hand backwards, reaching Aventurine's mouth just in time to shut off the explosion vibrating through her. By the third bedroom we passed, though, she'd reached a point of speechless fury. She seethed in silence, the stale air of the hidden corridor pulsing with her outrage.

Unlike her, I wasn't angry, but I was becoming more and more nervous – and not only about the conversations that we overheard. No matter how hard I looked, I couldn't spot a single golden, glowing light floating in any of the bedrooms that we passed. Where were they all? What were they doing?

I imagined them floating out like a golden net through the darkened outer corridors of the palace ... and then I stopped imagining that as quickly as possible, because that image – *glowing lights in the dark* – made my shoulders tighten with much-too-vivid memories.

I peered around the corner before I made my next turn ... and let out a sigh of relief when I didn't spot any golden lights floating towards us down the hidden corridor.

Whatever they were up to, at least they weren't doing it here. So we were still safe – for now.

The next stream of candlelight came from nearly twelve feet away, but I recognised the voice that travelled with it long before we reached the peephole. No one had a more distinctive sneer than the fairy crown prince, Franz.

'... You'd better get used to the flavour, little brother. Once you're married to the little rat, she'll probably insist you eat it every night!'

What?

'The fairies are marrying rats now?' Aventurine whisper-snorted. 'Typical!'

I waved a frantic hand to silence her as I pressed my ear against the wall a careful two feet away from the peephole.

They couldn't possibly mean ...

'She'll probably try to get you *reading*, too.' Franz gave a bark of contemptuous laughter. 'They say she thinks herself quite the philosopher, you know.'

Oh no.

No wonder the crown princess had sent Sofia out of the room for her negotiations with the fairy royals! She'd been negotiating her sister's betrothal to the younger prince, Ludolph ... and Sofia didn't know about it, I was certain. There was *no way* the grumpy princess would have stayed silent all afternoon and evening about *that* decision!

Of course royals always married other royals in the end. But I remembered the stiff, strained look on Sofia's face after her private conversation with the fairy princes earlier. The thought of her being sent to live with them underground when she grew up, with no sunlight and no fresh air and no way out ever again ...

Even after everything she had said and done over the past week, I couldn't help grimacing with sympathy. There were *some* advantages to not being a princess after all.

'I still don't see why *you* can't marry her,' Prince Ludolph muttered. 'It's not as if she won't come with a decent dowry.'

'You mean her dragons?' Prince Franz laughed. 'A dowry is supposed to last a girl throughout her entire marriage, remember? Those beasts won't survive a fortnight once Mama has them in her grip.'

What? My breath caught in my throat. Were they truly planning to *kill* Aventurine's family?

I'd known their plans couldn't be good, but this ...

Aventurine's low growl rumbled through the darkness. I grabbed her arm and squeezed hard to silence her.

'What was that?' Prince Ludolph's voice was sharp, and it grew louder as he approached the wall. 'Did you hear that? It sounded like –'

'You're imagining things again.' There was a soft thumping sound – Franz throwing himself down on to the bed perhaps? I could just imagine him crossing his long, glowing fingers behind his head and smirking at his younger brother. 'Too much time above ground and you start seeing enemies everywhere. Poor little brother, too scared to face the big, bad outside world. What was it that your future bride called you earlier, when you made that amusing little comment about her home? A "blind mole"?'

Oh, Sofia.

Naturally they'd taunted her into losing her temper – I'd seen that on all three of their faces when they'd arrived in the long gallery together. But if she didn't learn some self-control soon –

Prince Ludolph's growl cut off my thoughts. 'I'll show *you!*'

Footsteps thudded across the room, followed by a grunt. As the unmistakeable sounds of a scuffle broke out, accompanied by streams of strangely coloured light that shot through the peephole like fireworks, I clenched my teeth with frustration.

Talk now, fight later!

Panic was flaring like wildfire all across my skin, wanting to send me leaping head first into action, but I still needed more information. It wasn't enough just to know that the fairies wanted the dragons dead, no matter how sick with horror that made me feel. The crown princess already knew they hated Aventurine's family, and it hadn't stopped her from betrothing her own sister to Prince Ludolph. After all, she'd only allied with the dragons for their power in the first place. For all I knew, she might be happy to trade them for a stronger ally if the fairies offered her that choice.

So if I wanted to win back my place here, find my parents *and* keep my best friend's family safe, I had to learn exactly how the fairies planned to kill the dragons – and find a seriously persuasive reason why the crown princess couldn't go along with it.

And there was only one way I could discover any of that now that the fairy princes had stopped talking.

I remembered the fairy king's gaze resting thoughtfully on me earlier. '*My wife and I would quite like a word or two with this unusual Silke ...*'

A shiver of fear rippled through me.

I didn't want to spy on the fairy king in the darkness. Or on the queen either. The high, eerie, jingling sound of her laugh; the way she'd heard me even when I'd whispered ...

I remembered Marina's disapproving words when I'd first been hired. *Sending a thirteen-year-old girl to spy on a set of visitors who frighten the life out of any adults with common sense ...*

If the fairy royals caught me listening through their walls tonight ...

No! I shook the thought away, stiffening my spine.

I'd made my way through the guest wing undetected so far, hadn't I? A true heroine didn't give up halfway through her story just because she got a little scared.

Besides, what else was I going to do? Go running back to Dieter with my tail between my legs so I could cower in my tent and give up on ever seeing my parents again?

Never.

'Come on,' I whispered to Aventurine, and started forward.

She followed in simmering silence.

At the next turn in the corridor, I stopped.

Carefully, quietly, I tipped my head round the corner.

Nothing.

No glowing lights.

No candlelight either, to show where the peepholes were hiding. The narrow corridor was as black as obsidian ... or as the tunnels of underground Elfenwald.

I peered into the darkness, straining my ears for any fraction of a sound, but I couldn't hear a thing.

Had the fairy king and queen really gone to sleep already?

Maybe they'd blown out the candles but weren't sleeping yet. Maybe as soon as I got close enough to their peephole, I'd overhear them murmuring all of their wicked plans, in detail, to each other. Then I'd have everything I needed to save my parents, Aventurine's family *and* my lovely, safe position at the palace for evermore.

Even to me, it didn't sound a likely story. But it was the only story I had left tonight.

Holding my breath, I crept around the corner.

Total blackness.

Not a single golden light in sight ... and I was still at least fifteen feet from the next peephole.

I took one soft, careful step ... another –

Snick! A tinder struck in the darkness just before me.

Flame sparked into life.

'Boo!' A three-foot-tall, green-skinned creature, wearing a dark tunic and a bright red cap, grinned up at me with long, sharp teeth smeared red with blood. '*Got you!*'

CHAPTER 17

'Rrrr!' Aventurine charged forward.

My outflung arm stopped her just in time, even as the fairy's guard dropped one hand to the hilt of the long, curving knife that hung from his leather belt.

'Sir!' Inside, panic was rioting through my chest. But I beamed with all my might as I dipped into an awkward curtsey, still holding my best friend back with one hand.

Think fast!

'We must be here on the same mission,' I whispered to him.

The guard's eyebrows rose. His moss-green lips twitched. His small, strong-looking hand settled firmly over his knife hilt, which was coloured the same bright red as his cap ... and his teeth. *Ugh.* I couldn't let myself think any more about his teeth. Not unless I wanted to start gibbering.

'I doubt it,' he said, lowering his voice to match mine.

Aventurine snarled, '*Definitely* not. Goblins always do the fairies' snooping!'

Goblin? Well, that explained the green skin and his height.

Now I knew why I'd glimpsed all those flashes of red throughout the day. He must have sneaked in while the court was distracted with fairy jewellery and then spent the rest of the day watching everything, without us realising.

It was enough to send chills down my skin. *How much had he seen?*

And where had that blood on his teeth come from?

I intensified my smile, pushing all of those other questions out of the way.

'*What* an honour to meet you,' I whispered brightly. 'You must be one of Elfenwald's famous red-capped goblin guards!' I gestured grandly to the cheery velvet cap propped on his head. 'Why, everyone's heard stories of how impressive *you* are!'

'Mmm,' said the goblin. His hand didn't loosen its grip on his knife. But at least he hadn't pulled it out yet.

I shifted in front of Aventurine, who had her lips pulled back over her bared teeth and was letting out a low, ominous growl as she glowered at him. Luckily, I was a good five inches taller than her, so I could keep her expression safely hidden.

'The corridor's clear all the way behind us,' I whispered. 'Is it clear on your end, too? My mistress asked us to check that it was safe, for your comfort.'

'How ... thoughtful of her.' The goblin guard's eyes rested first on my white nightgown and bare feet, and then on Aventurine's garish turquoise-and-orange gown. 'I wouldn't have taken you two for palace guards.'

Aventurine snorted.

I shot one foot back and kicked her ankle.

'Oh, we're not guards,' I said. 'But I work for the princess –'

'Princess Sofia,' said the guard. 'I know. I saw you earlier.' His green lips curved into a wide, knowing grin. 'You're the storyteller.'

'Um ... ?' I blinked to a halt.

'I heard the story you told the fancy folk, earlier. An adventure and magic tale of the highest order.' He tipped back his large head to study me, his eyes dark pools of shadow. 'We respect our storytellers in the deeps. Do they honour you up here, storyteller, in the way that you deserve?'

In the tiny golden circle of candlelight, with darkness surrounding us on all sides, his square green face looked ageless and eerily still, like an ancient fortune teller waiting to tell me my future.

It took Aventurine nudging my back with one pointed finger to break my trance and make me stumble back into speech.

'I'm fine!' I said hastily. 'I mean, I'm one of the princess's ladies-in-waiting, and –'

'And now you're trying to sell me one of your stories,' said the goblin. 'We would pay you in fresh-cut jewels for that in the deeps, and drape your cavern in the softest green moss to show our appreciation.'

'She doesn't want any stupid moss.' Aventurine pushed free of me to glare down at the goblin with her arms crossed. 'She wants you to let us go, *now*. And don't go running to your tricksy masters to tell them all about us either!'

'Oh no?' The goblin guard's eyes narrowed. 'I know what she is,' he said softly. 'But I don't know what I should tell them about you. All I know is what you smell of, little girl: chocolate ... and *dragon*.'

Aventurine let out a ferocious snarl.

'*No!*' I lurched forward. 'She's not ... I mean, she's –'

'Oh, I know,' said the guard. '*Chocolate so sweet, it brokered a brilliant treaty.*'

Argh! Was there anyone in Elfenwald who *hadn't* read my handbill?

I had never meant to buy this kind of publicity.

His eyelids never blinked as he held Aventurine's burning gaze. 'How much time have you spent with those monsters, chocolate girl, ever since *your* masters made that treaty?'

Aventurine's mouth dropped open in thunderstruck outrage.

I seized the opportunity.

'Chocolate!' I whispered and softly clapped my hands together. 'That's it! Why don't you come down to the kitchen with us now, and we'll make you some lovely chocolate of your own? Aventurine makes wonderful hot chocolate. Everything *always* feels better when you drink it.'

And if I could talk my food-mage friend into using some persuasive magic on the hot chocolate she made for him, then within half an hour, he would forget ever having met us.

It would be *perfect*.

But the goblin was shaking his head, his voice rueful. 'I would have enjoyed that, storyteller,' he told me. 'But I have made a bargain, so I must serve my masters just as you both serve your own.'

'I don't have any *masters*!' Aventurine muttered.

I said, 'Wait!'

But he wasn't listening to either of us.

The rapping of his long, knobbly fingers against the wall echoed up and down the hidden corridor like a drumbeat of doom.

'What's going on out there?' the fairy queen demanded, her voice querulous and faint through the distant peephole. 'Alfric? Is that you?'

'Uninvited visitors, my queen,' called our guard. His voice lowered as he turned back to us. 'A pity.' He slid off his cap and gave a low, respectful bow in my direction. 'May the memory of your stories live long in your listeners' hearts.'

'Bring our visitors to us.' It was the fairy king's voice, pouring through the wall to resonate along the corridor with an unnatural power.

As I looked into Alfric's regretful gaze, I was filled with a cold, sick certainty: I wasn't going to be able to talk myself out of this one.

But Aventurine *smelt of dragon*. I couldn't take her in there!

Grabbing my friend's arm, I turned to run.

Too late.

Golden balls of light swarmed into the corridor from both directions. They whirled in a flashing, dazzling cloud all around us, pushing us closer and closer together and nearly blinding me as they swooped past my face.

As Aventurine batted at the sparking balls, the wordless roar that ripped out of her throat didn't sound even remotely human. In fact ...

Oh *no*.

I twisted round, desperately peering through the mass of whirling golden lights to the floor beyond, where Aventurine's shadow ought to lie.

Lights flashed past at high speed. I had to blink and blink again, with dark aftershocks flickering against the inside of my eyelids.

But through all the flashing confusion, I could just make out the shadow of a giant tail lashing furiously against the floor.

No, no, no!

'Aventurine!' I grabbed her shoulders and stared down into her feral golden gaze. 'Chocolate. Hot chocolate. Chocolate creams!'

She twisted in my grip, swiping at the balls of light

that whirled closest to her face. Her upper lip peeled back to show her teeth.

Could the goblin guard see her through the lights?

No, wait. The *lights* could see her! They were going to report everything to their masters and then they'd take her away, just like they'd taken my parents.

'Aventurine, look at me!' My eyes were burning, but I refused to blink. I *had* to hold her gaze, no matter what. 'Marina will be in danger if you do this!' I tried to shake her, but her shoulders were too strong. 'Horst will be, too! And ...'

Stop. I slammed my mouth shut before the pathetic words could come out:

You can't leave me, too!

Two familiar balls of golden light shot through the rest to attach themselves to either side of my neck, vibrating against my skin with a high, buzzing keen that sounded almost as if they were panicking, too.

What did *they* have to worry about? They were about to be proven right in all of their earlier suspicions. They weren't the ones who were about to lose everything *again*.

'No *one's* hurting Marina or Horst,' Aventurine growled, her voice thick with draconic rage. 'Especially not any tricksy fairies!'

'They won't want to,' I hissed back, 'if you just *keep control*! We don't need teeth and claws right now. We need –'

'Yes?' A deep voice drawled the words behind me, low and amused. 'Tell me, my uninvited visitor. What is it that you need, exactly?'

I spun around.

The fairy king stood in the corridor like a shining star in the darkness. Beams of bright light radiated from the beautiful lines of his face, and his magnificent, full-length robes swirled around him against the dusty floor. His dark eyes glittered as they rested on us ... and then moved to study the corridor beyond.

He couldn't see Aventurine's dragon shadow all the way from there, could he?

It was the second time that the rulers of Elfenwald had held the future of my family in their grasp, in the middle of a dark night with eerie, glowing golden lights floating all around.

But I wasn't seven years old any more. I wouldn't sit back and stay silent this time, or be distracted by those two particular lights that were bobbing urgently against my face as if to warn the fairy king against me.

'Your Majesty!' I swept out the skirts of my nightdress and sank through the cloud of fairy sentinels into a deep, respectful curtsey.

Alfric had called me a storyteller, hadn't he? It was time to live up to that title.

'We are *so* honoured to have the chance to speak to you in private,' I said warmly. 'We carry an important message from my mistress, Princess Sofia –'

'Oh, but you don't really work for Princess Sofia, do you?' The fairy king tilted his head, his long, shining black hair rippling over one robed shoulder as he studied me. 'No, you have quite a different set of employers, don't you, *Silke*?'

'Um ... ?' My throat felt as dry as if all the old, forgotten dust in the corridor had risen into it at once. I swallowed desperately, my thoughts whirling. Did he mean that I'd once worked at the Chocolate Heart? Had the fairy sentinels worked that much out? Or ...

'The dragons planted a spy in the royal palace,' the king said softly. 'And look – she came straight to us, our first night here. What a delightful welcome gift – even better than everything I had planned.'

His lips curved into a smile. He nodded to someone past my shoulder, and I suddenly realised that we'd been surrounded while I wasn't looking. The fairy gentlemen-in-waiting were assembled around us now – even Karl, who dropped his gaze when I looked at him – along with a second goblin guard, who watched us with an impassive gaze and a long knife shining in her green grasp.

'Tie up the chocolate girl so she can't alert anyone,' the king told his entourage, 'and bring the spy inside with us. She's going to give us exactly what we need to destroy the dragons.'

CHAPTER 18

I didn't even try to run. Instead, with my heartbeat thrumming against my throat, I said, 'Don't worry, Aventurine, it'll all be *fine –*'

But *no one* threatened Aventurine's family without a fight.

Her roar of fury blasted through the air.

I'd thought that nothing could ever budge the solid walls of this palace, but as Aventurine erupted into her full form, the narrow corridor buckled and crumbled around us.

Screams and shouts broke out from the fairy gentlemen-in-waiting as they scrambled out of the way of flying mortar. Golden balls of light shot outwards through the chaos – all except for my own particular pair of lights, whose high-pitched keens nearly deafened me as they hovered against my neck, vibrating hotly against my skin.

They might have been determined to hold me captive for their rulers, but I wasn't even thinking of escape. All I cared about was the gigantic, terrifying, reptilian beast who stomped, roaring and thrashing her tail at the centre of the chaos.

'Aventurine!'

Plunging forward, I ducked and rolled with my arms wrapped around my head, and landed safely beneath my best friend's massive, armoured body. Chunks of mortar tumbled around us. Her giant, taloned feet planted themselves firmly on the ground on either side of me, and her crimson-and-silver wings flared wide, reaching well into the room beyond. Her long, twisting neck reared high above through the broken ceiling as she bellowed, '*You aren't taking her anywhere!*'

What? Shock lanced through me, freezing me in place as I gaped up at her.

Aventurine wasn't defending her family right now.

She was trying to protect *me*!

I didn't have time to be staggered or grateful or furious. For once, I didn't even feel the urge to speak ... because as the dust cleared from the air, the fairy king and his entourage stood revealed beyond the piles of rubble in the hidden corridor, where Aventurine's big left feet were still planted.

Her right feet had landed in the next room over, a spacious, grandly decorated bedroom fit for royalty, with a canopy bed nearly as large as the Chocolate Heart's whole kitchen. Rubble had shot into the room when half the wall had collapsed inwards, but the centre of the floor was clear, and the fairy queen stood there, glowing like an irate star, sending fierce white beams of light into the air as she glared at us with glittering, sparkling eyes.

Stories wouldn't help us now. Only one thing could.

'Aventurine!' I smacked my hands hard against her massive, scaled chest, but she was too solid. I couldn't push her. '*Run!*' I ordered, pointing to the windows.

Her wings flared even wider with outrage, and I gritted my teeth, forcing my brain to work. 'I mean ... I need you to get *me* to safety!'

That did it. Her head swooped down towards me, all fifty giant teeth bared and gleaming with menace. I leaped on to her long crimson-and-silver neck and wriggled all the way down on to her hot back, digging myself in just behind her shoulder blades and between her wings, with my two irritating fairy lights still buzzing wildly beside my ears.

It wasn't easy to find a safe handhold, even without that horrible, humming distraction. Everywhere I looked, I saw rips and tears in Aventurine's beautiful scales where flying chunks of mortar had landed. They were all the reminder I needed of how vulnerable she was, despite her frightening appearance. It took a hundred years for a dragon's scales to fully harden, and until then ...

'You two aren't going anywhere!' Queen Clothilde flung out her shining hands.

A web of sparkling silver light sprayed across the room.

It tangled in Aventurine's outstretched wings, and she roared with fury and with pain, twisting wildly in its grip.

I lunged forward to peel it off, but it was as sticky as paste and burned icy cold against my fingers, in horrible counterpoint to the heat of Aventurine's big body. Blue-black bruises popped up against my skin everywhere I touched the wicked magic web, and a whimper of pain tore out of my chest as I worked. But I couldn't stop trying to pull it free, because Aventurine's vulnerable scales sizzled with steam at every spot the web touched – and as Aventurine twisted to get clear, her long neck tangled more and more in the sticky, icy web.

But her snout was still free. She opened it wide – and a jet of flame shot across the room, blasting through the web of light and heading straight for the fairy queen.

Clothilde leaped aside with a shriek of anger. Fire sparked against the closest wooden pole of her big canopy bed and spread downwards in a hissing, burning path that caught against the queen's glittering robes before she could move fully out of reach. Ha!

As the queen bent over to frantically slap out the flames, Aventurine yanked the web free with a roar of triumph – and as I clung to her back, I glimpsed a massive hole in the web's centre where my friend's flame had torn directly through it.

'That's it,' I breathed. 'Fairy magic can't withstand dragonfire!'

'But immature dragon scales cannot withstand our magic,' said a cold voice behind me.

The fairy king stood, panting and dishevelled, just out of reach of Aventurine's lashing tail, with tiny chunks of plaster and mortar tangled in his long black hair and scattered across the shoulders of his robe.

It should have been funny to see the elegant king in such a state. But it wasn't. As I watched his beautiful face glow with deadly light against his dark hair, I wanted to curl up and disappear, to keep him from ever taking notice of me again.

But it was much too late for me to blend in now.

His glittering gaze rested on my face as he began, slowly and unhurriedly, to raise his shining light-brown hands.

All the fairy gentlemen-in-waiting gathered behind him, forming a semicircle of glowing support. Karl's eyes were wide and panicked now, his cheeks flushed and his gaze sliding away from mine, but that didn't stop him from taking his place in the formation.

The fairy king's smile was full of satisfaction.

'We've dreamed for centuries of catching a helpless, infant beast', he told me. 'But we never imagined being handed such a gift unasked for. And you, *spy*?' His lips curled with sudden, fierce amusement. 'You brought her to our very doorstep. You will be remembered in our court *forever*.'

Forever?

I looked into his glittering dark eyes and gave up every hope that I'd had left for my own future. As dozens of glowing balls of light whirled at dizzying speed through

the room, and my own particular two lights buzzed frantically against my ears, there was only one thing I could do.

'Aventurine,' I told my best friend, 'burn it *all* down.'

Aventurine reared back on her hind legs and opened
her vast mouth wide.

The fairy king and queen both threw up their hands
to attack ...

And the still-standing door to the outer corridor flew
open with a bang that sent it crashing against the elegant
striped wallpaper.

'What in the *world* is going on here?' demanded the
crown princess.

It was the first time I'd ever seen Princess Katrin looking
less than perfect. Her magnificent lavender dressing gown
was embroidered with gold-and-silver thread, but it was
wrapped around a plain nightdress. Her dark, curly hair
hung in a long plait down her back. She must have
scrambled with undignified speed across the palace to get
here as quickly as she had – and as she stalked into the
room, half a dozen royal guards marched after her, clanking
with enough weaponry to fight a battle.

But Princess Katrin cast her gaze across the wreck of
the room with the unshakeable assurance of a woman who
knew that she owned everything she surveyed ... and
wasn't at all pleased about what had been done to it.

'This palace has stood for nearly two hundred years.'

Her gaze rested on the smashed-in wall and the piles
of rubble, then shifted, without haste, to the burning bed

in the far corner. The flames had already spread from the first bedpost along the upper canopy and rumpled covers, and they were burning merrily along all four bedposts now.

'Has it occurred to anyone here', she asked, 'to put out that fire before it destroys any more of my family's ancestral home?'

Aventurine closed her mouth with a guilty snap that echoed across the room.

Even the fairy king and queen lowered their hands, although the queen's face was twisted with rage.

It was the fairy king who spoke, his voice cutting like a blade of ice through the smoky air as servants bustled forward from behind the royal guards to attend to the flaming bed.

'Has it occurred to your family', King Casimir asked, 'to protect your guests from attack in their beds? Or were your words of peace and negotiation merely a clever ruse to deceive us so that the dragons, *your allies*, could finally devour us just as they devoured so many of our family members in the past?'

The crown princess seemed to gain a full inch in height as she stiffened with outrage. Her gaze flicked swiftly across the room, from the giant hole in the wall that had formed when Aventurine had crashed through it, to the bed where her servants fought against the flames ... and finally to me, sitting atop Aventurine's scaly back, with the tangled remnants of Queen Clothilde's magic web hanging all round us.

Oh, *mud*.

Had she heard me telling Aventurine to burn it all down?

I sat up straighter on Aventurine, nudging her back down on to all four feet.

'Your Highness.' I tried for an air of dignity in my nightdress. 'This was not an attack.'

'Oh no?' Her eyebrows lifted as she pointedly surveyed the wreckage. 'A friendly meeting then?'

Queen Clothilde let out a muffled shriek. 'Do you really expect us to stand about chatting? We were set upon in our rooms by your cousin and that monster! Will you do nothing to avenge your guests?'

Aventurine let out a low, threatening growl that made half the people in the room jump. With her lips pulled back over her long, sharp teeth, she really did look a bit like the monster they had called her ... and as everyone else edged away from us, I could feel the situation slipping away from me.

If I had learned one thing in the last week, it was that ladies-in-waiting were never allowed to contradict royalty. So it turned out to be a good thing after all that I'd been sacked earlier this evening.

'Their Majesties are ... mistaken,' I said through gritted teeth. It was the diplomatic way to say 'they're lying', and everyone knew it. Even the footmen who were busy emptying buckets of water over the bed turned to stare at me.

With a high-pitched keen, the two golden lights zoomed forward to hover in front of my face, as if they were saying to their fairy masters: 'You see? We told you not to trust her!'

I plunged onwards, even as Aventurine's muscles bunched underneath me, clearly bracing for oncoming battle. 'Neither of us intended any harm to your guests. But when *we* were attacked by the king and his guards in the corridor outside, Aventurine changed shape in self-defence. It wasn't –'

'Self-defence?' The fairy queen's eerie laugh seemed to signal that something even worse was coming. 'You two were skulking around inside our walls like rats. Do you hope to convince anyone that you *weren't* planning to attack us while we slept?'

'We weren't,' I said. 'Truly! Your Highness –'

The crown princess's expression looked as if it had been set in stone. 'Well?' she said. 'What exactly were you doing behind their walls ... cousin?'

I looked into her face and the words dried up, unspoken, in my mouth: *We were spying for you.*

She would never publicly admit the real reason she had hired me ... and tonight, she could tell the fairy royals with perfect honesty that I hadn't even been working for her any more.

A small cough sounded at the side of the room. Alfric the goblin guard slipped through the crowd of fairy courtiers, his sudden appearance making the crown princess's eyes widen and the fairy queen's eyebrows shoot up with unmistakeable outrage. 'Ahem,' he said. 'I believe your cousin may have mentioned a message they were carrying for Their Majesties? From the younger princess, she said.'

He was actually coming forward to help us, after working so hard *not* to be seen ever since he'd arrived in the fairies' wake. I almost let out a sob of laughter at that realisation.

Of all the people in this palace, he was the one I'd least expected to have as an ally now.

I knew for certain, though, exactly what would happen if Princess Sofia were roused from her bed and asked to vouch for me in front of everyone.

I *think not.*

I lifted my chin and met my former employer's gaze full on for the last time. 'Forgive me,' I said quietly, under the gaze of the fairy royals. 'We were only curious – we meant no harm. There was no message.'

'No,' Princess Katrin said with icy clarity. 'I thought not. Now, cousin ...' her lips twisted as she turned away, '... you and your *curious* friend are both dismissed. You may both leave this room, this palace *and* this city. I do not wish to see either of you in Drachenburg ever again.'

CHAPTER 19

Leave this city? My city?

I couldn't even go back to the riverbank?

My chest felt as if it were filling with thick, poisonous lead as the crown princess turned away from me.

Six years of learning every street in Drachenburg, embedding myself so deeply in the heart of it that I could never, ever be forced out again ...

Four nearly sleepless nights and days of preparation in this palace, and so many years of glorious dreams leading up to them ...

'Yes, Your Highness', I whispered through numb lips. I shifted over to the edge of Aventurine's back, preparing to slide off.

But the fairy queen spoke over me. 'I think not!'

Golden balls of light flew towards her from all four corners of the room, as if in answer to an inaudible command. They gathered around her in a shifting, growing cloud, as she continued, 'Do you imagine a mere *exile* is punishment enough to satisfy us?'

Uh-*oh*. I'd been about to swing my legs off Aventurine's back, but I stilled as I absorbed her words.

Aventurine radiated dangerous heat, like a furnace getting ready to explode.

My two personal golden lights retreated to hover by my hair, vibrating even faster than before. Their high, anxious hums rose to a pitch that pierced through my head like a knife.

Even the crown princess went still for one long moment as the fairy queen's words hung in the air. Then she turned, and I sucked in my breath as I took in the expression on her face.

The royal guards stepped into place behind Princess Katrin, shoulders squaring. There were no battle mages in sight, but I would have wagered anything that they were on their way, summoned from their quarters across the palace.

If they didn't arrive in time ...

'I *beg your pardon*?' the crown princess said.

Queen Clothilde snorted. 'Don't try to overawe me, little girl. You may have your dim-witted father under your thumb, but I've been ruling my own kingdom for longer than you've been alive. You can't placate me with a mean-ingless show! You order that vicious beast out of this palace, and she'll go straight back to her family's lair with everything she's learned about us tonight. We'll be attacked before dawn by the adults in her pack!'

Aventurine snarled, 'My family wouldn't waste their breath on you!'

The queen sneered back at her. 'As if I'd ever believe a word you said, *animal!*'

'*There will be no attack.*' The crown princess's gritted teeth sounded through her words. 'Our allies had no interest in this visit. They offered, in fact, to keep a safe distance throughout all of your time here so as not to alarm you –'

'A safe distance?!' Queen Clothilde waved at Aventurine, dislodging fairy lights from the cloud around her with every movement. She swung her arm in a sweeping gesture to indicate the broken wall and the soaking-wet bed whose flames had finally been put out. 'Does any of this look *safe* to you, young lady?'

'Princess Katrin.' King Casimir crossed the room with slow, deliberate strides as golden balls of light flew in dizzying circles round his robes.

The only lights not gathered around their masters now were the two just by me, and their humming grew more and more ear-piercing – almost as if they were in pain themselves – as they clung closer and closer to my neck, resisting the royals' call.

The fairy king's lips curved into a smile that filled me with dread. 'My dear,' he said gently to the crown princess, 'you must know you have no real choice. You *will* turn over the beast and her companion to us. There is no other decision you can possibly make. Why prolong this awkward moment any longer?'

'Our allies –' she began.

Queen Clothilde spat out her words. 'Your allies are *beasts*.'

'Your allies,' said King Casimir, 'are here in this room with you.' He held out his hands, gracefully indicating the fairy courtiers who stood behind him. 'Oh, we may have danced about the matter in our earlier negotiations, but you're a clever girl, Katrin. You must have guessed by now that you'll have to choose between us. And who, exactly, *will* you choose to present to your people as favoured partners? Those fire-breathing monsters who terrify everyone – and who aren't even here to stand by your side now? Or ...'

He snapped his fingers, and more jewellery cascaded through the air behind him, clattering on to the floor in a priceless shower of gold and rubies and sapphires.

'... Choose us,' he finished softly. 'We can make *all* of your courtiers and citizens so much happier through our alliance, and bring your kingdom wealth beyond your wildest dreams.'

No, no, no!

My breath was coming in deep, rapid gasps.

For one flashing moment, I was back in that market hall in the fifteenth district, surrounded by angry, frightened traders. '*Who knows how long until they start eating us?*'

I couldn't read the crown princess's expression, but I

didn't need to. If I knew how much her people feared Aventurine's family, so did she.

So if I didn't come up with something fast ...

'Your Majesties!' My voice came out as a near squeak, but I forced it to lower as I summoned a desperate smile for the fairy royals, breaking through the silent battle of wills that hung in the air. 'There's no need for any threats or unpleasantness! Aventurine and I will happily agree to be confined in the king's prison here in Drachenburg for the rest of your visit, to reassure you.'

Aventurine swung her head around to glare at me, letting out a disgusted puff of smoke from her big nostrils, but I narrowed my eyes at her as I said, 'We'll *both* let ourselves be locked up without a fight. Then you won't have anything to fear from the other dragons – we won't be able to report to them! – and you can safely enjoy the rest of your visit without –'

'Pah.' Queen Clothilde rolled her eyes. 'As if any human prison could hold that creature. No, there is only one possible solution.' She smiled at the crown princess, her eyes sparkling with a thousand lights. 'You'll simply have to turn our attackers over to us, as a mark of your goodwill and the seal upon our new alliance. We will look after them ourselves, for *all* of our sakes. And then we will negotiate our own agreement with the dragons for their safe return.'

Aventurine's murderous growl rumbled through the room. This time, I couldn't blame her.

I *liked* Aventurine's family, massive and fire-breathing

though they might be. They'd always treated me kindly, as Aventurine's friend – and arrogant and territorial as they were, it would never even enter their hard heads to break an alliance they'd sworn to for any reason. They were too honourable for that.

But they would do anything to protect their hatchling. The idea of what the fairies might demand of them in exchange for Aventurine's life filled me with dread. If they were tricked into trying to negotiate our safety, only for the fairies to ambush them in some way ...

The fairy king's earlier words rang in my ears. '*She's going to give us exactly what we need to destroy the dragons.*'

'Don't do this,' I said hoarsely to the crown princess.

I didn't have any cleverness left. Only desperation.

Don't let me be responsible for destroying Aventurine's family.

'Please!' I said. 'You signed a treaty with the dragons. You can't break it now.'

'Oh, really?' Clothilde smirked. 'What do bargains mean to humans?' She waved one hand in impatient dismissal. 'Now –'

'Katrin?' An unexpected voice spoke from the doorway. It was Princess Sofia, bundled up in a satin dressing gown and holding a candle. For once, she was alone, without a single lady-in-waiting in sight. Her expression brimmed with panic as she looked, wide-eyed, from the destruction of the back wall to me and Aventurine, to the fairy queen and her cloud of golden lights ... and finally to her older sister. 'What's been happening here?'

'Go back to bed, Sofia.' Katrin snapped out the words without looking away from the fairy royals for an instant. 'You don't belong here.'

'Nonsense.' King Casimir gave Sofia a smile that made goosebumps run up and down my arms. 'Why shouldn't our future daughter-in-law be included in this conversation? After all, this may well be her dowry we're negotiating.'

'What?' Sofia gasped.

The crown princess winced. 'Sofia ...'

'Quite right,' said Queen Clothilde. 'In fact, we may as well bring her back with us tonight.'

'Tonight?' Katrin asked sharply. 'But –'

'Why not?' The fairy queen shrugged. 'There's no need for us to remain above ground any longer, is there? I believe we have everything we need now. Give us twenty minutes to round up our children and the more lag-abed attendants, and we'll be safely home within an hour.'

An hour? To get all the way to Elfenwald?

One of the crown princess's guards let out a startled cough.

The awareness of fairy magic seemed to fill the room until I was choking on it. Could even battle mages win against it? They might be able to do magic, but these fairies were magic, and I was finally beginning to understand that difference.

'No one's taking me anywhere!' Sofia snapped. She was breathing hard, and she might have been trying to look haughty, but panic was written all across her face. 'Katrin, tell her!'

'Do tell her,' King Casimir invited the crown princess. 'With tonight's agreement, your sister will unite both of our ancient kingdoms and bring untold wealth to your little nation through our generous trade agreements ... just as we discussed this afternoon.'

Sofia's mouth dropped open. The expression on her face, as she stared at her sister, wasn't disbelief.

It was terror.

'You can't,' she whispered. 'You can't send me underground with them. *Please.*'

'What we discussed,' Katrin said tightly, 'was a *preliminary* betrothal, with the wedding intended to take place years from now, after Sofia has finished all of her training and education. Her departure tonight, with no warning and no time to say her farewells, was never mentioned or agreed –'

'Oh, but it is essential that she be trained by us.' Queen Clothilde sniffed. 'Trust me, it will be difficult enough for our court to accept a mere *human* princess as Ludolph's match. We've wasted far too much time already – really, we should have had her handed over when she was first born, if we'd only realised how useful this connection could be.'

Sofia let out a wordless moan. Her free hand clutched her opposite arm, as if to hold herself in place. Her wide brown eyes never left her sister's face. 'You promised me,' she whispered. 'You promised *Mother*. Katrin –'

'Your sister,' the fairy king said softly, 'knows as well as we do that we could never trust any alliance without the surety of your presence in our own court. Otherwise, what would keep her from breaking her agreement with us, just as she's turning her back on the dragons now?'

'Humans,' said Queen Clothilde, 'can never be trusted unless they're *forced*.'

Sofia's face drained of colour until she looked nearly grey beneath her light brown skin. 'Katrin,' she whispered, her voice broken.

For the first time since Sofia had arrived, the crown princess looked at her younger sister, her expression as calm and impenetrable as always. 'Of course,' she said. 'What could please me more than to hand my own sister over to such a safe and loving new home, where she will be valued so highly? I'm sure I can trust your new parents to look after you properly, Sofia, after tonight's fine showing. What better allies could I hope for indeed?'

Wait. What? I had to stop my eyebrows from shooting up. The fairy royals were nodding and smiling, but there was something in the crown princess's tone ...

Princess Katrin tilted her head, stepping sideways until she stood between the open door and the fairy royals' view. 'Sofia? Go and join our cousin now.'

'Our ... ?' Sofia's eyes looked glassy with shock as she stared at her sister. Tears slipped silently from her eyes and rolled down her cheeks, but she didn't even try to wipe them off.

'Well?' Imperiously, the crown princess pointed towards me. 'Don't you think you ought to prepare yourself for your journey?'

Ohhh.

My hands clenched round Aventurine's neck. The heat from her scales burned against my bruised fingers. '*Get ready*,' I whispered.

Sofia moved towards us with slow, dragging footsteps, her gaze turned inwards. 'But ... Father ...' Her voice came out as a bare thread of sound.

'We'll summon him now,' said her older sister. 'You know he always takes my lead on such matters. I'm sure your new family won't mind you taking the time to say farewell before you leave.'

'Of course not.' Queen Clothilde smiled triumphantly. 'But you needn't bother to have any of your ugly clothes collected while you wait. We'll supply you with *real* fashion once we're safely underground. Oh yes, we'll have all the time in the world to teach you the ways of a proper court over the next few years before your marriage.'

'Sofia has always been an excellent student.' The crown princess shifted, drawing both the king and queen's gazes with her, as a flicker of black showed just beyond the open door, like a shadow made of cloth ... or a battle mage's robe. 'In the meantime, we have agreements of our own to seal before you leave. My guards will keep the captives under control for you while we negotiate, I assure you.' She gave a rapid, fluid signal with one hand to the captain of her personal guard, who nodded with military precision.

As the three adult royals huddled together, human guards in blue-and-silver uniforms marched up in a line behind Sofia, spreading out until they separated her – and us – from everyone else in the wreckage of the room. Sofia didn't even seem to notice them behind her as she trudged across the floor, her shoulders slumping more and more with every step.

Holding my breath, I looked above Sofia's bowed head and met the eyes of the captain of the guard. Her pale, freckled face was tight with tension, but the smile she gave me was fierce.

'Your Highness', she said to Sofia, 'allow me to assist you.'

'Wha–?' Sofia's voice cut off in a startled grunt as the captain scooped her up. 'How dare you – *oof!*'

She landed with a thud on Aventurine's broad, scaly back, just behind me.

I yanked Sofia's arms around my waist. '*Now!*' I hissed.

Aventurine's powerful hindquarters gathered underneath me. Her wings snapped out. With a triumphant roar, she lunged forward, straight towards the nearby windows.

Fairy voices rose in sudden outrage behind our wall of guards. Metal clanged through the air as our defenders drew their swords. Half a dozen black-cloaked battle mages burst into the room through the open door, chanting with all their might. As the room descended into utter chaos, one voice rose above all the rest: the fairy queen, letting out a vengeful shriek.

'*You stupid little girls!* You will regret this!'

The fairy lights by my ears keened in unmistakeable panic. Magic shivered through the air behind me.

Aventurine's big body crashed through the windows

and the wall around them, sending glass and rubble flying in our wake. Shards of glass showered around me.

Sofia's scream of terror filled my ears. Her arms squeezed painfully tightly round my stomach.

Blood-curdling yells sounded from fairies and humans alike ...

And I let out a whoop of pure relief as we sailed out into the cold, dark night air, leaving the ruined royal palace behind us.

CHAPTER 20

My relief lasted for less than five seconds. Then I realised that we were falling through the darkness.

'Aventurine!' I shrieked. '*Use your wings!*'

'*I'm trying!*' Aventurine bellowed back.

'Aaaahhhhhhh!' Sofia screamed into my ear as we plummeted.

The ground zoomed towards us as Aventurine's massive wings flapped wildly, sending wind buffeting across her back. I pressed the side of my face against her neck and clung on for dear life. Candlelight flared in the windows of the palace around us. Shocked faces appeared at the glass, but they were much too far away to save us as the paving stones rushed closer and closer and –

Whoosh! We were suddenly rising through the air in

wavering dips and bobs that sent us careening through the stone courtyard, this way and that, as people flooded out of the building on to the ground below, shouting and pointing up at us and at the massive hole in the wall above us where the battle was still taking place.

At least Sofia had finally stopped screaming. Instead, she said in a voice shredded by fury, *'Take me back!'*

'Not for all the gold in a dragon's hoard,' I told her. 'We – *oof!'* We had just knocked into an unbroken part of the palace wall with a thump that nearly shook me off my perch. 'Careful!' I gasped as I scrambled for balance.

'Trying!' Aventurine snarled. *'I've never done this before.'*

Uh-oh. I tightened my arms around her broad neck as Sofia's arms tightened convulsively around my waist.

'You've never flown before?' the princess screamed. 'But you're a dragon!'

'She's a *young* dragon,' I yelled back as we veered danger-ously close to the next wall. 'It's – *oof!* – not her fault if no one's taught her how to do it yet. *Oof!*' I gritted my teeth as we took another stomach-mangling swerve and sudden drop.

'Argh!' Sofia wailed. 'I cannot believe my sister ever hired you two!'

'There you are!' A cold, triumphant voice filled the courtyard.

The fairy queen stood in the opening in the broken palace wall, with light flaring behind her and multi-coloured sparks flying off her tall figure in all directions. Her pale, glowing face creased into a smile as she drew back both hands with clear intent.

'Aventurine!' I said. 'The web!'

'Grr!' Aventurine flipped to one side and shot upwards so fast my stomach felt as if it were dropping out of my body.

Even as I clung to her neck for safety, I craned my own neck to peer downwards. The wicked magical web shot towards us in a stream of glittering white light ... that landed in the darkness just below the end of Aventurine's tail. It fell harmlessly to the ground.

Phew.

As the queen let out a jagged scream of fury, my two personal golden lights pulled away from my neck with a high, keening sound of protest. They flew back towards their queen like homing pigeons ...

But the rest of us were free. Aventurine's wings beat strongly through the air, carrying us high over the palace roof and leaving the courtyard far below. I laid my head against her thick, strong neck and let out a long, shuddering breath, letting the comforting heat of her scales pour through me and ward against the cold night air.

For the first time since we'd exploded out of the palace, I could hear a steady, rhythmic beat in the pattern of my best friend's flight. We weren't wavering or wobbling any more. She'd finally worked out how to use her wings properly.

We were safe.

Aventurine must have come to the same conclusion. Her whole body tilted forward, trading her fierce, nearly vertical push upwards for a smooth, horizontal path high above the palace. As we flew over the long sweep of the south-east wing, I shifted upright into a sitting position and shook out the tight muscles in my shoulders.

Stars sparkled serenely above us. We were a part of the night sky now, too, high above all the lights and battles and dangers below. No one could reach us any more. We were flying! I threw my arms out to my sides, balancing on Aventurine's broad back, and I let out a laugh of sheer delight as the long, loose sleeves of my white nightgown billowed in the wind.

If only Dieter could see me now!

Then Sofia spoke behind me. 'What are they going to do to my sister?' Her voice wasn't high and furious any more. It sounded small and tight and breakable.

Oh, *mud*. My arms sank back down to my sides as I let myself think through everything I'd seen.

The fairy queen could never have reached that opening in the wall if she and her husband hadn't defeated all of the crown princess's guards and battle mages first. Which meant ...

'They won't kill her,' I said as confidently as I could. 'Royals *never* kill other royals, you know. They have rules about that.'

Although when it came to everyone else in the room ...

I remembered the fierce smile on the face of the captain of the guard as she'd thrown Sofia to safety. My stomach clenched.

Maybe the guards and the battle mages were fine, too. After all, the fairy queen didn't need to kill them, did she?

She could just wrap them up in her magic web to keep them still. That was definitely what must have happened.

Probably.

But I couldn't let myself think about that any more. So I said as brightly as I could, 'I'm sure your sister will have the situation under control soon enough. She'll hold them off while we go and get Aventurine's family. Now that we have you safe –'

'*Safe?*' Sofia let out a laugh like broken glass. 'First, you two smashed in the walls doing who-knows-what, and then you kidnapped me before I could even agree to what the fairies wanted! You're the whole reason everyone's in danger right now!'

'You think we *kidnapped* you?' I twisted around, peering through the darkness in disbelief. 'We just saved you! Remember?'

If I'd ever expected gratitude from a princess, I'd been mistaken.

'You fool!' Sofia yanked her arms free from my waist. 'If you hadn't panicked and flown away with me, Katrin could have used me as her bargaining chip! Once she'd arranged all the details of my betrothal, they would have forgiven her for the disaster you two caused, even if you did run away afterwards. Then –'

'Your sister wanted us to take you with us,' I said. 'Didn't you even notice any of her signals? You *asked* her not to let them take you, remember? She was protecting you, just like you wanted.'

And I could still barely believe it. I'd never even

imagined the crown princess choosing anyone else's happiness above the good of her kingdom. Whatever promise to their mother Sofia had referred to, it must have been a powerful one – or else there was far more to the sisters' relationship than I'd realised.

Either way, Sofia could at least try to be grateful!

But I bit down hard on my tongue to hold that thought back. *Diplomacy. Courtesy. Remember them?* Those skills were essential for mingling with royals, even on dragon-back.

'You know *nothing* about me or my sister,' Sofia hissed. 'What would you know about families? You don't even have a real *home.*'

That did it.

I'd spent the last four days keeping my hands folded and my opinions to myself, until I'd nearly suffocated under the weight of blending in. Now I'd failed in my mission after all that preparation, I'd lost my final chance to save my parents, I'd seen my best friend attacked and nearly captured by fairies, and I'd – mostly accidentally – destroyed the royal palace.

Every single one of my dreams was as broken as the wall we'd left behind us ... and, apparently, my tact had just shattered, too.

'*I'm* not the one who doesn't understand your sister!'

Sofia gasped. 'How dare you?'

'No,' I told her grimly. 'How dare *you*? You've done nothing but make my life difficult for *days*, all because you were jealous that your sister gave me a job you weren't even *remotely* suited for! You're so desperate to impress her, but you never go about it in the right way. And now that she's finally chosen you over everyone else in the kingdom, you're shouting at *me* like a toddler having a temper tantrum!'

'I ... wha– *what?*' Sofia's mouth gaped open. 'You're not allowed to talk to me that way! No one is!'

'Oh, forget court rules', I snapped. 'We're not in the palace any more. We *broke* the palace, remember? And now we're your sister's only hope of rescue, so maybe – just possibly! – you should learn to be polite to other people yourself, *Your Highness*, no matter how worthless and lowly you think we all are.'

Sofia stared at me for a long, fraught moment as the cold air rushed past us and Aventurine flew over the roofs of the city, her wings beating steadily on either side of us.

Then the princess finally muttered, 'I don't think you're worthless.' She sniffed loudly, and finished in a miserable undertone, 'I think I am.'

What?

Muffled, snorting noises emerged from behind me.

Before I could even imagine what to say in response, Aventurine gave a sudden lurch in mid-air. I slid forward and sideways in a horrible, slippery rush.

'Argh!' I flung my arms around her neck just in time to save myself from tipping into the air. My heartbeat thundered in my ears as I clung on with both arms and legs, panting hard.

'Sorry', my best friend called back in a low, grumbling

roar. 'My wings aren't used to flying yet. We'll have to take a break.'

'What, *here*?' Sofia's voice sounded froggy with snot and tears, and I felt a damp patch where her face pressed against my back. 'But we're still in the middle of the city!'

I looked down over Aventurine's broad neck and sighed. 'I know where we can land safely,' I told them.

But I really wasn't looking forward to it.

By the time we circled down to the riverbank three minutes later, I'd managed to pull myself back up into a sitting position, I'd brushed the last shards of glass out of my hair, and I'd straightened my nightgown as well as I could. As all of my old neighbours flooded out of their tents, staring and exclaiming and pointing up at us in the dancing light from the communal firepit, I fixed a broad, confident grin on my face. I even waved cheerily at them in greeting as we landed on the snow-dusted ground.

Nothing wrong here! This is a perfectly normal way for me to spend my evening.

But it wasn't enough.

Of course it wasn't.

As I met my brother's gaze through the crowd of onlookers, his eyes widened in shock ... but only for a moment.

Then Dieter sighed and shook his head, his shoulders sagging in resignation as he stepped forward.

'Oh, Silke,' he said. 'What have you done this time?'

CHAPTER 21

This wasn't how I'd imagined returning from my royal adventure.

I *had* planned to come back for a visit, of course, once the fairies were safely gone, so that I could tell the story of my fabulous victory to everyone who'd listen. Naturally, I'd be wearing my finest court clothes, and I would arrive in a grand carriage with at least four horses. I might be accompanied by a personal maid, and I would definitely be carrying my first month's salary as the crown princess's official right-hand girl, the one she could count on to do *anything*.

Then my older brother would finally, *finally* have to realise how wrong he had been about me!

Well.

As I looked down at him now, I sat astride a dragon, wearing a floor-length nightgown that had picked up dark smudges and a long, ragged tear along the hem. My face and arms were covered with cuts from flying glass. My fingers and palms were still sore from touching that burning-cold fairy web, and every time I lifted my hands off Aventurine's hot scales, the cold air made my bruises throb like new all over again.

I slid off Aventurine's back with a thump and landed barefoot on the snow-dusted riverbank.

Squelch.

My feet sank into cold, wet mud up to my ankles.

Sniffs and murmurs ran through the gathered crowd. I ignored all of them and kept my eyes on my brother.

'Don't worry,' I told him. 'We won't be staying long.'

'You ...' His lips pressed together hard and his face twisted as if he were trying to hold back some strong emotion. Then he gave a quick glance up at Aventurine's back and his mouth dropped open. 'Your Highness!'

He dropped to one knee on the muddy ground.

Gasps sounded throughout the onlookers. Moving as one, all of my gossiping, disapproving old neighbours lowered themselves deferentially to the cold, wet mud as Sofia slid down off Aventurine's back after me, looking every inch the haughty royal that she was.

In the flickering firelight, I couldn't make out any sign of the tears that I'd heard from her during our flight. Her eyelids might have been a bit puffier than usual, but her chin was jerked up just as arrogantly as ever.

... And she was actually wearing shoes! I could have murdered her for those, as the freezing cold mud between my bare toes sent shivers rippling up and down my body.

'Quick!' a voice called urgently from the crowd. It was Frieda, the one who'd always sniffed the loudest whenever she'd seen me leaving the family market stall for new adventures. 'Someone bring a blanket for Her Highness! She must be cold!'

Seriously? I gritted my teeth together to keep them from chattering too loudly. Had no one even noticed that Sofia had a gorgeous dressing gown wrapped around her nightgown? She was probably the warmest person there!

'Your Highness.' Frieda's husband, Hanno, hurried towards us, carrying a quilt that I recognised immediately.

Frieda had spent over a year haggling scraps for it from everyone who sold clothing on the riverbank, arguing fiercely for all of the clothes that she insisted were too ragged for us to sell. The finished quilt was packed full of deliciously warm duck feathers, and the sight of it bundled up in Hanno's arms made a whimper of need rise up through my throat.

'Here.' Bowing – and keeping his gaze turned away from the massive crimson-and-silver dragon who crouched nearby – Hanno held the quilt out to Sofia. 'Please. Wrap yourself in this, Your Highness, and come closer to the fire while you tell us all how you came to honour us with your presence. I beg you will accept our most heartfelt apologies for any –' he sighed as he glanced at me – '*inconveniences* you may have experienced from any of our riverside family along the way.'

'Thank you,' Sofia muttered.

She took the quilt from him, but she didn't follow his beckoning gesture towards the firepit. Instead, she stood with the warm quilt piled in her arms and her head lowered, worrying at her lower lip ... until she finally swung around with a gusty sigh and held the quilt out to me.

'Silke's the one who should have this,' the princess said. 'She saved all of us tonight. Well, Aventurine did, too.' She waved at my best friend's looming, reptilian figure. 'But *she's* probably warm enough already – you know, dragon heat.'

'*Aventurine?*' Dieter had met my friend Aventurine-the-girl-from-the-chocolate-house at least a dozen times by now, but I'd never shared her real history with him. He swung towards her now, staring. 'But ... how –?'

'I'll explain everything later. I promise.' I bit back a moan of relief as I swirled the big quilt around my shoulders and its cloak of warmth surrounded me. Just as I was about to wrap the corners tightly around my neck to anchor it, though, my gaze landed back on Princess Sofia.

Her arms were crossed at jagged angles. Her square chin jutted out as she scowled at the ground, ignoring the curious gazes aimed at her from every occupant of the riverbank.

She couldn't have looked more arrogant or more sulky if she'd tried.

But I remembered words mumbled almost too quietly for me to hear during our flight, and my shoulders rose and fell in a reluctant sigh.

'Here.' I held out one arm to her, opening the quilt around me. 'We'd better share it for warmth, don't you think?'

She held still for a long moment. I braced myself for the scathing response that was sure to follow.

Then she gave a jerky, one-shoulder shrug. 'I suppose so,' she muttered. 'If we have to.'

A few minutes later, we were settled on wooden chairs side by side in front of the firepit, with Frieda's quilt stretched around both of our shoulders. It didn't cover my whole body, of course – it wasn't *that* long – but the fire burned steadily, and Aventurine settled her big head on her foreclaws nearby, breathing a constant stream of hot air that swirled around my legs and surrounded me in warmth and safety.

Dieter, Hanno and Frieda sat across the firepit, but the rest of the crowd had finally, reluctantly, withdrawn. They certainly weren't asleep, though. Most of them seemed to have found one excuse or another to poke around the outsides of their thin tents. Everyone in the camp was listening as hard as they could to every word that we spoke.

This wasn't the story I had wanted to tell any of them. But with my older brother and two of our most disapproving neighbours all waiting for an explanation, I didn't have much choice but to launch into it.

'... So we crashed through the wall and flew away,' I

finished several minutes later. 'Now Aventurine and the princess are safe, but –'

'Goodness, child, what are you thinking? You're not safe,' said Frieda. 'Do you think no one noticed you landing here?' She shook her head, *tsk*ing loudly. 'We're still not used to dragons flying overhead in this city, you know!'

'I know.' I grimaced.

At least no one here seemed too terrified of Aventurine. Everyone had kept a safe distance from her when we'd first landed, but now that she was lying sprawled across the riverbank, her scaly eyelids drooping and the tip of her snout resting close to the fire, most people barely even bothered to skirt her bulky tail as they moved about their business between the tents.

Of course, we were used to unusual new immigrants on the riverbank.

Also, a thin trickle of drool was oozing out of Aventurine's big mouth as she half dozed by the fire. It was hard to feel too frightened of anyone who was sleep-drooling, no matter how large or scaly they might be.

'That's why we can't stay long,' I told Frieda. 'Well, and we need to go and get help, too, of course.'

'Against the fairies?' Dieter hadn't uttered a word since I'd begun my story. He'd only hunched his shoulders tighter with every passing minute. Now, though, the words burst out of him like an explosion. 'We barely escaped from them six years ago. Now you've walked right back into their midst on purpose?'

'Dieter –' I began.

'Without even *telling* me?'

'I tried!' I gritted my teeth. 'You wouldn't listen. You never –'

'After everything our parents sacrificed to save us from them last time? After –'

'Wait, what?' Sofia had been slumped beside me, listening without contributing, but now she jerked upright. 'You two have met the fairies before? In Elfenwald, you mean?'

Frieda let out a huff of air through her nose and pressed her lips together, looking down at her pale, gnarled hands.

Hanno coughed pointedly.

'Silke didn't even tell you?' Dieter shook his head as he turned back to me, his voice dull with a despair that burned against my bones. 'You really don't care about our family any more, do you?'

'Of course I care!' I nearly yelled. 'Why do you think I went to work for the crown princess in the first place?'

'*What?!*' Dieter and Sofia both exclaimed the word at the same time in identical tones of horror.

I was gripping the quilt so tightly now, it was in danger of ripping. But so what if it did? I'd already ruined everything else tonight. Breaking one more cherished, precious thing wouldn't make a difference.

'I wanted to save them,' I snapped, 'even if no one else in this camp ever bothered to try!'

Frieda sucked in a hissing breath through her teeth. Outrage thickened the air around us.

'Child –' Hanno began heavily.

Before he could finish, Dieter jerked his chair back from the fire. Without another word, my brother turned and stalked away from me, out of the firelight and into the darkness.

The quilt shifted around my shoulders as Sofia turned to face me. She didn't speak.

She didn't have to. Her expression said it all.

Oh, *fine*. Maybe she wasn't the only one who didn't know how to handle her older sibling. But who cared? Who cared what any of them thought?

I jerked my chin higher and tucked my bare feet closer to the heat of my best friend's massive red-and-silver snout.

'Well?' I challenged Hanno. 'How else would you describe what happened in Elfenwald?'

Wrinkles creased my neighbour's face as he let out another sigh, suddenly looking years older. 'It was all a very long time ago,' he said quietly. His gaze fell to his hands, which were clenched tightly on his knees.

Frieda's pale, knobbled right hand landed on top of his. 'It's old business.' She scowled at me ferociously. 'It is *done*.'

'But it's important now,' said Princess Sofia. All of her sister's cool authority rang in her voice as she straightened in her seat, tugging the quilt along with her like a royal robe. 'Tell me,' she ordered them. 'What exactly happened to Silke's parents in Elfenwald?'

CHAPTER 22

'It all happened more than six years ago,' Hanno said. Something crackled loudly in the firepit between us, and he leaned forward to stir the logs, looking down at them as he spoke to Sofia. 'You know about the troubles up north?'

'Of course.' The princess sniffed. 'I learned about them from my tutors ages ago.'

'Well, then.' He took a deep breath as he straightened, rolling out his shoulders. 'You'll know, then, that your parents issued a proclamation declaring refugees welcome if we could only find our way here to their protection. So we packed what we had left and fled – men, women and children all together in one long wagon train. More and more of us joined along the way.'

'And you came through Elfenwald?' Sofia frowned.

'Why would you take such a stupid risk? It wasn't even your most direct route. It must have taken ages longer to go that way round.'

'Hmmph!' Frieda shook her head, drawing her shawl closer around herself.

Hanno put one big hand on her knee. 'No one wanted to go that way,' he said mildly. 'But not all rulers were as welcoming as your father ... and there were those who thought that if they allowed us through their borders, we might never leave again.'

'They sent their thugs out to turn us back,' Frieda said sharply. 'That's what he's trying to say. Every bully boy who ever wanted to feel strong came loping out from their village to stop us. They blocked our way, stole all the valuables we had left and threatened to do worse if we didn't go back to where we'd come from.'

'But we couldn't go home. So ...' Hanno's shoulders rose and fell in a shrug. 'We had to take the risk, in the end. We voted on it and agreed.' For the first time in the story, his weary gaze landed on me. 'We *all* agreed,' he told me. 'Your parents both voted to take the Elfenwald passage. Your mother argued passionately for it when the rest of us were faltering. She and your father would have risked anything to bring you children to freedom.'

Then why wouldn't anyone risk anything for them?

I set my jaw and glared into the fire. Flames popped as the logs shifted. Thick smoke streamed through the air to water my eyes. Aventurine's head tilted on her foreclaws, and she let out a low, rumbling growl in her sleep that made Hanno and Frieda both give a nervous start.

'Don't worry about her', Sofia said impatiently. '*She's* not dangerous unless you insult her chocolate'. She leaned forward, pulling the quilt with her and pulling me with it. 'Keep going with your story. What happened when you crossed into Elfenwald?'

Hanno and Frieda exchanged a look. As I watched, they inched closer to each other on their seats.

'Nothing', Hanno said, 'at first. We travelled all that first day without meeting a soul'.

'They were watching us, though'. Frieda shivered. 'I felt it. We all did'.

'Perhaps'. Hanno grimaced. 'But it was deathly quiet. No animals or birds in the woods around us. No people, ever. And we knew better than to camp overnight. But that evening ...'

'Golden lights in the darkness', Frieda whispered. 'And a bargain'.

I couldn't help it. A convulsive shiver rippled through me, and the faces across from me turned blurry. I was seven years old again in that dark wagon, with dancing golden lights all around us ...

No. I wouldn't be pulled down into panic again. Those lights in the palace hadn't managed to hurt me, had they? We'd got away from all of the fairies when they'd tried to take us tonight.

And I couldn't afford to miss any details of this story – *especially* the parts I'd never heard before.

'What bargain are you talking about?' I asked.

And why hadn't I guessed that one must have been involved? Those fairies had been talking about bargains all day.

I remembered Alfric, the red-capped goblin guard, in the secret corridor that evening. '*I have made a bargain, so I must serve my masters ...*'

My fingers dropped away from the quilt as I sucked in a breath, looking from Hanno to Frieda's pinched face. 'What *bargain* did you all make to sacrifice my parents?' I whispered.

'It wasn't us who made the bargain,' Hanno told me. 'They did.'

I jerked forward, but Sofia grabbed my arm.

'Quiet,' she told me, tugging me back down. 'I want to hear this.'

Next to me, I felt Aventurine's big head move. When I glanced down, I saw that her eyelids had flicked open. Her golden eyes were steady and alert.

I wasn't alone. Not any more.

'Fine.' I settled back into my seat, but none of the warmth from the quilt or from Aventurine's breath could stop the shivers rippling through me. 'Tell us all the story.'

'They were everywhere,' Frieda said. 'Everywhere!' She threw her arms out. 'One moment we were alone in the woods, and then those lights appeared all around us ... along with *them*.' Her face tightened. 'They appeared on the path in front of us. Their skin ...' Her hands came back together, fingers clenching in her lap. 'Even their eyes shone in the dark.'

'They called us spies,' Hanno said heavily. 'It didn't matter what we told them. They said we must be after their silver, or working for dragons ...' His eyes slid to Aventurine, then shifted quickly away. 'They said they would lock us all underground, where we couldn't give away their secrets. When we argued – when your father said he wouldn't let them take his children anywhere ...'

Raised voices – I remembered. And then our mother leaping out of our wagon with a sudden cry, leaving me and my brother behind.

'*Dieter, look after Silke ...*'

'It was your mother who saved us all.' Frieda's lips twisted into something that only resembled a smile. 'She always did have a gift with words. The stories that she used to tell you two children when she put you to bed every night! Half the camp used to put off their final chores just to listen in. Silly stories, really ... but I always listened, too. I couldn't help it.'

My eyes were watering again, but this time, I didn't wipe the tears away. I let them slide down my cheeks, and I lifted my chin, refusing to hide them.

These tears belonged to my mother. She deserved every one of them.

'She tried her best to persuade the fairies of our innocence,' Hanno said. 'If anyone could have managed it, it would have been her. But when she finally realised it was useless, she tried other tactics ... and then, in passing, she happened to use the word "bargain". He shook his head wonderingly. 'How they all went still when they heard it!'

'It was the first time I felt any hope', Frieda said. 'It was the first time they'd paid attention.'

'So she asked what bargain she could offer them to let our company go', Hanno told us. 'And they conferred together for a moment.'

'They said she would have to be the one to pay it', said Frieda. 'She and her husband, too, to punish him for what they called his *impudence* in trying to refuse them in the first place.'

My fingernails bit into my palms. 'What bargain?'

'One hundred years of service', Hanno said.

'One hundred?' I stared at him. 'But –'

'Perhaps fairies have longer lives than us.' He sighed. 'Or perhaps they knew exactly what they were asking. Your parents certainly knew they could never survive to the end of their commitment. But your safety was worth the sacrifice to them.'

'*Our* safety?' I wasn't crying any more. Rage filled me too hot and full for tears as I threw down the quilt that I'd been sharing. 'What about *their* safety? They were your friends! Why didn't any of you argue?' I lunged to my feet to glare down at them. 'Why didn't anyone say no?' I demanded. 'Why didn't you all come together and fight?'

'Because there was no point!' Frieda snapped, glaring back at me. 'Haven't you been listening to any of this?'

Next to me, Aventurine's lips pulled back from her long teeth. I could actually feel her vibrating with aggression beside me. To a dragon, that decision would be unforgivable – but this time, her fury couldn't hold a candle to my own.

'Of course there was a point!' I shouted. 'I don't care if you thought you couldn't win! The *point* was that you don't let your friends go without a fight! The point was –'

'No,' Hanno said firmly. 'They were already gone by then.'

'But –'

'Wait.' Sofia's voice sounded strange and strained. When I looked down at her ...

Was that *pity* I saw in the grumpy princess's face?

Surely not.

'I think ... I think I might know what happened, Silke. From what I've read ... if I'm right in what I've guessed ...'

'It happened the instant that your parents said "yes",' Hanno told me. 'The torches all went out a moment later, but first ...'

'We all saw it.' Frieda wrapped her arms around her waist, looking haunted. 'It happened right before our eyes.'

'Our friends were gone in less than a heartbeat,' said Hanno. 'In their place ...'

The fire crackled. I stared down at him, my mouth open and my mind racing.

No. No, no, no, no ...

'Two more golden lights in the darkness,' Frieda finished. 'You see? There was no one to go back for.'

No one to go back for.

I barely felt myself collapse back into the rickety wooden chair.

I didn't feel the heat from the fire or the chill from the air.

All I could feel was the roiling of my stomach and the throbbing in my head as I finally, finally realised the truth.

Hanno and Frieda and all the rest of the adults I'd always blamed had never had a chance to save my parents.

But I had, today. I had!

Two golden lights buzzing frantically around me all day long...

They hadn't been singling me out to show their rulers. They'd been trying to tell me who they were. In the end, when they'd flung themselves in front of my face just when their rulers were about to attack ...

How could I not have guessed? They'd been trying to protect me.

I had *had my parents back* for nearly a full day of my life without realising it ...

And I had flown away from them without a second glance.

I knocked the wooden chair out from under me and lunged barefoot across the snowy, squelching mud of the riverbank.

Voices rose behind me, blurring together in agitated protest, but I ignored every single one of them as I ran as fast as I could back towards the broken palace and my parents.

I couldn't leave them behind again.

CHAPTER 23

It was Dieter who stopped me, his tall, skinny figure suddenly looming out of the darkness ahead.

I slammed into his chest before I could stop myself. Then I tried to twist away from him, but he grabbed my arms.

'Silke!' His fingers tightened as I struggled in his grip. 'What do you think you're doing?'

'*Let me go!*' I ground the words through my teeth as I threw my weight forward. There weren't any clever, persuasive arguments left in me.

I had to *run*.

My brother staggered, but it wasn't enough. His breath ruffled against my hair as he let out an infuriatingly weary sigh. 'I don't know what mad lark you're off on now, but if you think you can just leave your dragon friend and the princess here for *us* to deal with –'

'They're not the ones I left behind!' I bared my teeth at him, feeling feral. '*Our parents* are in that palace, Dieter! Right now! I left them there!'

His mouth dropped open. 'W*hat?*'

For the first time, his hands loosened. I jerked free ...

But someone else had already caught up to us.

'Well?' Aventurine was grinning her fiercest and most dangerous grin. Smoke trickled out of her big nostrils as she loped up beside us on all four feet, leaving massive claw prints in the snow and mud behind her. 'If you're going into battle, you're not leaving *me* behind. You still don't have any real teeth of your own, you know. And you can't breathe fire without me.'

I looked up at my scaly, ferocious best friend, ready to fly back into danger for me with no questions asked, and a wave of emotion hit me so hard that I started to shake. I had to wrap my arms around my chest to hold it all in and stay standing.

'Thank you,' I whispered. 'Thank you so much. But –'

'Wait!' Sofia was panting as she ran towards us, Frieda's quilt wrapped around her like a cloak. 'You can't just go running back there without a plan! Come on, Silke. T*hink.* You're supposed to be good at that!'

Was I? I blinked hard, trying to clear my head. But all I could think of were those two golden lights buzzing around me all day long, trying so desperately to communicate with me ... and that high, keening noise of pain that they had made as they'd been ripped away in the end. I hadn't even *tried* to keep them with me.

I had to press my lips together to hold back a moan of grief and fear.

'Is she telling the truth?' Dieter's voice sounded young and lost as he turned to the princess. 'About our parents? In the palace?'

'Yes, yes.' Sofia waved impatiently at him. 'We don't have time to explain all that again. You would have heard all the details already if you hadn't walked off in a huff. You really ought to listen to your sister, you know! Even *my* sister thinks she's clever.'

For once, I couldn't even bring myself to enjoy my brother's shock.

'The point is,' Sofia continued sternly, 'we barely made it out of the palace in the first place. If we just go running back into it now, we'll be caught within seconds. So what exactly *are* we going to do to save your parents and my sister and father?'

For once, her hectoring tone didn't grate on me. Instead, it cut through the thick fog of panic and grief in my mind, helping me to see clearly again.

Right. I took a deep breath, anchoring myself. My feet were half sunk in the cold, squelchy mud. Nearby, I could hear the quiet voices of other members of the camp moving busily around their tents, along with the familiar *swish-swish* of the river flowing past.

I knew this riverbank. I knew this city. And now I knew the palace, too.

I had spent all of my life preparing for this moment without ever realising it.

I'd been waiting to save my parents all along.

'You're right', I told her. 'We can't go in through any of the front doors.'

'Good start.' Sofia nodded in condescending approval. 'So?'

'This is a waste of time', Aventurine growled. 'If you two think we can't deal with the fairies on our own, all we have to do is go and get my family to help. We'll come roaring in from the mountains and –'

'No!' Sofia and I both said at once.

'Why not?' Aventurine shot a puff of smoke from her nose, looking as fed up as I'd ever seen her. 'The fairies are scared of dragons! Didn't you hear them?'

'But they have my sister and father', Sofia said. 'They'll use them as hostages if they see any dragons coming.'

'And they have my parents', I added, 'along with all of the other humans they've trapped and turned into their sentinels over the years. That's why so many people disappeared forever after they stepped into Elfenwald – they're the ones the fairies would send out to face the dragons first, before they ever risked themselves.' I shook my head, my right fingers tapping a rapid beat against my left elbow as my thoughts shot through dozens of different possibilities and discarded them all. 'Besides, Marina and Horst and loads of other people are still in that palace. We don't want any of them getting hurt. Sofia is right. We can't just fly straight in, roaring and breathing fire to attack. We have to be clever about this.'

Aventurine let out a huff of aggravation. 'What's the point of a battle spent *talking* about things?'

'It's what I'm good at', I told her. 'Just like my mother.' Next to me, Dieter let out a stifled sound through his closed lips. I lifted my chin and looked past him at Aventurine. 'Besides, you're not just good at fighting, remember? I think it's time for you to turn human again.'

'With fairies around?' the princess demanded. 'What are you talking about? Her fire is the only thing that can cut through their magic!'

'But she has magic of her own when she's a human', I told her. 'Chocolate magic. I think it's finally time to use it.'

With a whirl of light and colour, Aventurine's big crimson-and-silver body collapsed in on itself. A moment later, my best friend stood facing me, small and fierce and golden-eyed in her ugly turquoise-and-orange dress, with her arms crossed in front of her and her short black hair sticking out around her face.

'It's useless, though', she told me. 'You'll never talk them into drinking my chocolate. Not tonight.'

'They don't need to', I told her. 'Wait and see.' I turned to the princess, my hands falling to my sides. 'Do you want to stay safe here? I'm sure someone would lend you a tent if –'

'Hmmph.' Sofia snorted and tucked her quilt more carefully around herself. 'Don't even think about leaving me behind. That's my palace you broke!'

I rolled my eyes at her, but I couldn't help giving her a genuine smile for the very first time in our acquaintance.

215

'Fine. Your Highness can come along on our fabulous adventure party, then.'

'I should think so.' She gave a tiny smile back to me.

Bracing myself, I turned back to Dieter, who'd stayed silent and stunned throughout our conversation. His shoulders were hunched, his face looked hollow and wounded ... and for once, I really didn't want to argue with him.

It was so late. It was so dark. And the memory of my mother's final words was still ringing in my ears: '*Dieter, look after Silke.*'

A pang of longing sliced through my chest as I looked up at him.

I wanted back the brother that I had had once, long ago. The one who'd held me safe when we'd first lost our parents, as our wagons had hurtled away through the darkness. The one who'd argued so desperately with the grown-ups as we'd begged them to turn back.

... The one who'd promised me, crying and stroking my hair, that he would be strong and keep me safe no matter what; that we would always be each other's family.

There had been so many years of arguments since then – ever since we'd reached this city and I'd found my own, separate dreams, carrying me away from him. Dieter would never understand them or me; I would never get that old big brother back.

But I couldn't bear to leave him with a hateful argument again.

So I forced myself to smile as I looked into his

wounded face. 'Don't worry,' I said gently. 'I'll bring them back safe. I promise.' *Somehow.*

'No.'

'No?' I closed my eyes as a wave of exhaustion overwhelmed me. 'I know you don't think I'm good at anything, but –'

'No,' Dieter repeated. 'You're not leaving me behind. Not again!' As my eyes shot open, he swallowed visibly, his Adam's apple bobbing up and down his long, skinny throat. 'I thought I *had* to let you go last time. But I can't keep on doing it. I can't keep on watching my family walk away from me, again and again. I can't survive it!'

'Dieter ...' For once, I didn't know what to say.

But he did.

'So I'm coming with you,' he told me, 'and we'll all get them back. Together.'

Half an hour later, the four of us emerged from a maze of alleys and side streets into the first district. The street lamps were lit, but the curving, cobblestoned street that lay ahead of us was empty except for a few ragged men sleeping on doorsteps.

'What are we doing here?' Dieter hissed behind me as we hovered at the edge of the final alleyway. In front of us, a line of closed shops hulked against the darkness. 'I thought we were going to the palace.'

'We are,' I whispered back. 'Trust me. Sofia? I'll need the guards inside to see you first, so they don't do anything foolish.'

'Like stabbing us, you mean?' Aventurine asked drily from my left.

'*What?*' said Dieter.

'Oh, fine.' Sofia let out an irritable sigh and stepped in front of me, finally pulling off Frieda's quilt. Tossing it to me, she strode forward. 'I've already walked through all the smelliest alleys in this city tonight. I might as well –'

'Wait!' I lunged forward and grabbed the thick sleeve of her dressing gown, yanking her back into the alleyway.

'*What –?*'

Aventurine clapped one hand over Sofia's mouth.

Together, ignoring the princess's muffled protests, we pulled her into the shadows, close against the alley wall.

... Just as three golden lights floated into view above the cobblestoned street.

Dieter, still standing exposed in the centre of the alleyway, sucked in a much-too-sharp breath.

The golden lights hovered for one long moment at the alley's entrance. Then one separated from the rest to float through the darkness, aiming directly at my brother.

He stood as stiff as a statue as my hands clenched around Sofia's sleeves. He didn't even seem to breathe as the light lazily circled around him, slowly inspecting him from his waist upwards. There was no hum of delight this time; this light was only looking for information ... or for *us*.

But there was no reason for it to recognise my older brother. I told myself that again and again as I watched, holding my breath.

I *couldn't* move to save him. I couldn't ...

It gave up a moment later and abandoned him, floating back out of the alleyway on to the main street. The three lights circled each other then flew on, disappearing from view.

I met Dieter's gaze through the shadows.

He didn't say a word. But he gave me a small, tight nod.

We waited in silence for two long minutes before I finally dared to move.

One sliding, silent step ... another ...

'They're gone.' I let out my breath as I looked down the street.

The street lamps still cast a golden glow over the snow-slick cobblestones. The shops were still dark. The homeless men on the doorsteps still slept.

But now we knew that the fairies had taken over more than just the palace.

CHAPTER 24

None of us spoke as we slipped across the road. The fairy sentinels could be back at any moment – and no matter how they'd been forced into this position, they were well under the fairies' magical control now. Even my parents hadn't managed to resist the royals' call for long.

I couldn't let them find us. But I couldn't keep the air from rattling in and out of my mouth in harsh, panicky breaths as I picked my way across the snow-and-muck-covered cobblestones in the too-tight boots that Dieter had found for me in our stall's collection.

The door of the bookshop, of course, was locked.

Argh. I groaned inwardly as I pushed down on the handle. It didn't budge even when I rattled it with all my might. The broad glass window showed nothing but pitch-darkness inside the shop.

So much for being quiet!

It took three terrifyingly loud, hammering sets of knocks before I even glimpsed faint candlelight in the building's second floor. Then the window above us finally opened, and an older woman glowered down.

'Who on earth would make such an unholy racket at this time of ni– Your Highness!' She gasped as Sofia stepped out into the light from the street lamps. 'I – what –?'

'Quickly!' I hissed, almost dancing with impatience. 'Open the door!'

Her head disappeared, and the window shut.

'Phew.' Sofia joined us on the doorstep, huddling close. 'I hope it's warmer inside.'

I bit back the words: *We have worse things to worry about.* If the fairy sentinels were making regular rounds of the first district's streets ... How many sentinels *had* the fairies brought with them on this visit anyway?

I almost fell through the door when it finally opened.

'Hurry!' I pushed Sofia in before me as the bookshop owner hastily stepped out of our way. Then I hurtled in after her, pulling Aventurine with me. Dieter closed the door behind us and turned the long key in the lock.

'Can we cover up this glass?' he asked, frowning uneasily at the big window at the front of the shop.

'What?' The owner gaped at him.

'Don't worry about that!' I said, bouncing impatiently on the toes of my borrowed boots. 'But for heaven's sake, put out that candle!'

'You want me to stand here in the dark?' the owner demanded. 'Of all the –!' She snapped her mouth shut, her chest rising and falling with the words that she was visibly repressing.

Then her gaze settled back on the princess's expectant face, and she heaved a heavy sigh. 'As you say.' Dipping a curtsey, she blew out the tiny flame. 'Is there anything else I can do to be of assistance, Your Highness?'

'That will be all,' said Sofia with regal condescension.

'In that case ...' She sighed again, even more pointedly than before. 'I'll leave you all in peace, I suppose.' Her dressing gown rustled as she stepped back.

'Wait!' I fumbled forward in the darkness and piled Frieda's quilt into the woman's arms. 'Would you look after this, please? It's ...' What would she think when she saw it in the light? It was only an old rag quilt from the riverbank. But still ... 'It's special.'

Of course, Frieda hadn't asked Sofia to give it back when we left. How could she? Sofia was our princess – and Sofia, equally naturally, hadn't thought twice about walking off with it. She'd spent her whole life being handed far lovelier things, all handmade with care, to use or discard at her pleasure.

I knew how long Frieda had worked on that quilt, though. And after all the years I'd spent thinking bitter, unfair thoughts about her, I wouldn't throw away her most precious possession now that I finally knew the truth.

There was a moment of startled silence. Then the owner spoke again, her tone a fraction warmer than before. 'Of course. I'll keep it safe until you return.'

If *we return.* 'Thank you.'

I reached out in the darkness to find the others' hands, until we had formed a human chain. 'This way!'

It wasn't easy to find our stumbling way. But every time I banged my shoulder into a towering bookcase or my hip into a hard table piled high with teetering stacks of books, I remembered: if I couldn't see where I was going, no fairy sentinels could see me through that dangerously big window.

When my hand touched the back door at last, I knew that it had all been worth it. 'Here!'

We tumbled all together into the secret passageway and closed the door behind us.

Phew.

'Halt!'

Less than a week ago, when I'd first stepped into this passageway with the crown princess's messenger, the two guards on duty had stood against the wall and watched us with their swords sheathed at their sides and their gazes impassive. Now they lunged to meet our party with wild eyes and swords held ready. Their lamp sat in a metal frame on the ground behind them, casting a small, vulnerable circle of light with dark shadows lurking all around it.

'Your Highness.' The guard in front lurched to a stop, waving his partner back as he recognised the princess. 'Forgive us. We thought –'

'I know.' Sofia's tone was surprisingly gentle. 'You thought we were invaders. What's happening inside, Jurgen?'

'I don't know.' He threw his shoulders back into a military position, his broad brown face hardening. 'Our duty is to guard this post, no matter what the circumstances. But –'

'There was so much shouting!' The second guard was younger, and his pale skin flushed pink as he spoke. 'Then it all stopped at once, as if ...' His voice wobbled, and he broke off to swallow hard. 'It just *stopped!*'

'Fairy magic,' Aventurine growled. The words sounded like a curse.

The shadows that lurked around our circle of light seemed to thicken, pressing in on us. The younger guard's sword trembled in his hand.

'Don't worry,' I told him. 'We have a plan.'

'What plan?' Dieter demanded. 'No one's explained it to me yet!'

I flashed him and the watching guards my most confident grin.

Sofia looked resigned; Aventurine was smirking.

'Don't worry about the details,' I told my brother. 'All we have to do now is find a way down to the chocolate kitchen without alerting the fairies along the way.'

'We'll escort you,' the older guard said immediately. 'Her Highness's safety is our highest priority.'

Aventurine rolled her eyes. 'You're not going to stop any fairies with those swords.'

'Never mind,' I said. 'You can be our lookouts.'

I wasn't leaving anyone behind in the dark. Not tonight.

We all emerged into the crown princess's private, hexagon-shaped meeting room only a few minutes later. There were no golden lights floating in there, thank goodness.

The younger guard opened the outer door and peered past it, then beckoned us forward. 'It's safe.'

No, it's not, I thought as I slipped through the doorway after him.

The corridor was pitch-black, it was true, without a single golden light in sight. But we wouldn't be able to retreat into the hidden servants' corridors until we reached the map room, two doors down. And even there ...

I remembered the cloud of lights that had come swarming down both sides of the secret passage behind the fairy royals' rooms earlier. My spine tightened nearly to cracking point.

Nowhere in this palace was safe any more. The thick, heavy silence that blanketed the corridor ahead felt even more ominous than jingling fairy bells. The royal palace was far too busy and crowded to ever be completely silent, even at night ... until now.

What had happened to all of the courtiers and servants and guards? Why couldn't we hear anybody in the distance?

I would have given any amount of dragon gold to put out the guards' lamp. The glow that it cast – lighting all of us as we moved in a tight, rustling group – felt like a *look at me!* signal to every fairy sentinel who might float idly past the end of this corridor. But there were too many of us in our motley group now, and I was the only one used to slipping around in the dark. If anyone knocked into something or fell over, the noise could bring sentinels flying from every corner of the palace.

Every footstep that sounded – every heavy breath or hiss of air between someone's teeth – seemed a thousand times louder as it fell into the listening darkness.

I forced myself to breathe evenly and almost silently through my nose, my lips pressed tightly together, as I slid on my booted feet down the corridor, peering into the shadows ahead of me. Ten more feet to the map room ... eight feet ... five –

Something scraped against the floor nearby, just outside the glow of the lamplight.

'What's that?' the younger guard whispered loudly.

'Shhh!' I hissed back – then cursed myself, slamming my lips together. *No more noise!*

A low chuckle sounded in the darkness.

I knew that sound.

'Who's there?' the older guard, Jurgen, demanded. He shifted in front of Sofia, adjusting his sword in his grip, as the younger guard swung the lantern around, his eyes darting back and forth.

But they were both looking too high in the air.

As soft leather boots scuffed against the ground, I looked down to the level of my waist, already knowing what I would see.

Alfric's square green face was set in a rueful expression as he stepped into the circle of light. His long knife glinted

226

at his waist, and the bloody tips of his sharp teeth looked as dark as night.

'Ah, storyteller.' He shook his head at me. 'You should never have come back ... but my masters will be only too pleased to see you.'

CHAPTER 25

Aventurine growled and started forward.

Jurgen and his partner both swung around, gripping their swords.

Sofia gasped and Dieter let out a strangled sound in the back of his throat.

I took a deep breath for courage and waved them all back. 'There you are!' Smiling, I moved forward to meet the goblin guard halfway. 'I was hoping to meet you here,' I said with almost total honesty.

I had definitely hoped to meet *him* rather than any of the other goblins or fairies who might have been on patrol tonight. With them, I wouldn't have stood a chance. With Alfric, I had ... possibilities. But only if I could figure out exactly how to put all of the evening's puzzle pieces together.

'*Come on, Silke.* Think. *You're supposed to be good at that!*'

'Alfric,' I said, 'what would you say if I offered you a bargain?'

The air around us seemed to shiver.

Alfric's lips drew back into a dangerous smile that showed off the red tips of his pointed teeth. 'I'm listening.'

'Silke ...' Dieter began in a pained undertone.

'Shh!' I hissed. Then I turned back to Alfric. 'You told me earlier that your people would give me precious jewels for my stories,' I said, 'or ... or moss, to decorate a cavern of my own. Was that right?'

'Those would indeed be our first tokens of appreciation for such a deep honour.' He nodded gravely. 'But alas, I cannot offer you any of those gifts now. My masters have taken you as an enemy, and I must obey.'

'Because of the bargain that you struck with them.' I swallowed, my eyes searching the darkness beyond him. How long until a searching fairy light appeared at the end of the corridor? 'I'm guessing that you couldn't break that bargain even if you tried. Is that right?'

'Break a *bargain*?' His bushy green eyebrows lowered into a disapproving frown. 'Bargains are sacred and bound by the most ancient magic, young one. Have you lost even the memory of such commitments above ground?'

'We-e-ell ...' I drew a deep breath.

Aventurine shifted impatiently beside me. She didn't have to say a word; I knew exactly what she wanted: to stop talking and to fight, overpower him and move on. Eerie though he might be, with two soldiers and Aventurine's

229

claws on our side, Alfric on his own couldn't possibly stand against us.

But that was only because he hadn't summoned any sentinels to alert his masters yet.

I moistened my lips, choosing my words carefully. 'What if I offered you a bargain that wouldn't break your agreement with the fairies?'

'I would tell you to be very careful, storyteller.' Alfric gazed up at me, his eyes dark and ancient. 'I am sworn to protect my masters' lives, and I cannot put them in danger even for the greatest of rewards.'

Of course. The magic wouldn't let him.

That – as I'd worked out on my way back to the palace – was why fairies didn't trust humans or dragons to keep their bargains: dragons destroyed magic by their nature, and humans didn't possess enough of it in the first place.

And *that* was why human trespassers had to be transformed into a magical form before the fairies would trust their service. Only then could their bargains truly bind them.

'I won't ask you to put your masters in danger.' The toes of my boots pinched so badly that I had to tip back on my heels, balancing as carefully as I could. 'I don't want anyone to be hurt, not even them.'

'But,' said Alfric softly, 'I have been ordered to bring you to my masters tonight if I should happen to find you in my patrols. How do you reconcile *that* with your proposed bargain, storyteller?'

'I would say ... that sounds perfect!' As a wave of relief

rushed through me, I landed back on my full feet with a thud.

'What?' Aventurine grabbed my arm and peered at me suspiciously. 'Have you been enchanted by fairy magic, too?'

Dieter said anxiously, 'Could that have happened?'

'No!' I pulled free, rolling my eyes at them both.

The guards were watching me wide-eyed, still holding their swords ready, and Sofia's face was set in a considering scowl.

But I could finally feel the lightness of true hope rushing through me as I turned back to Alfric, balancing my words as carefully as I'd balanced on my heels a moment earlier. 'What if I told you that coming with us now, with just one stop along the way, would be the most efficient way to bring us to your masters? Especially if you don't let any of the fairy sentinels see us and slow us down? You'd save all of the time and effort it would take to have a long, noisy battle. And I promise to come with you quietly once I've made that single stop! It would be *so* much faster in the end, and in exchange for your help, I'll tell you a story of your own. So ... ?' I paused and moistened my lips, trying to read his expression. 'Would that be enough for us to strike a new bargain without breaking your first bargain with the fairies?'

He looked at me for a long, considering moment as I held my breath.

Please, please, please ...

When the goblin guard finally spoke, his voice was filled with the weight of stone.

'Rebellion will never work', he told me. 'No magic on earth can overcome my masters. In all of history, only full-grown dragons have ever managed to stand against them. Whatever hopeless heroics you may be planning for your-self now, they are doomed to failure and pain and misery. You would do far better to give them up and come quietly before you enrage my masters further.'

He sighed heavily, his green face lined with weariness. 'Be sensible, young one. You are only a magic-less human girl. You have no power with which to fight them ... and trust me: you do *not* wish to know what punishments they can devise for true impertinence.'

The younger guard gulped audibly. Dieter let out a muffled groan, Sofia gave an outraged sniff and Aventurine's menacing growl rumbled through the air.

I gave Alfric my most mischievous grin. 'Well then, why don't I tell you your story first, before we go to your masters?' I suggested. 'That way I can fulfil my end of the bargain *before* all of that inevitable failure and pain and misery. Agreed?'

For one tense moment, everything hung in the balance.

Then a sharp-toothed grin spread across Alfric's face. 'We respect bravery like yours in the deeps, storyteller, even when it is so utterly doomed.' Stepping back, he gave me a courtly bow. 'I have only one request as I escort you on your final journey to my masters: I wish my story to include Drachenburg's famous chocolate.'

'That should be absolutely fine', I said happily, 'because guess where we're going first?'

It was easy to find my way to the chocolate kitchen by the light of the guards' lantern, especially with a story to tell along the way. I'd mapped these corridors for hours in the dark, and with Alfric's help, we weren't seen by a single fairy sentinel the whole way. The look of wonder on his green face, as I told him a brand new story I'd invented just for him, was almost enough to make me glow like a fairy myself with satisfaction.

I might have failed at many things tonight, but storytelling was something I really did know how to do.

Unfortunately, I didn't get to savour that feeling for long.

'Horst!' said Aventurine as she stepped into the darkened kitchen ahead of me. Then she stopped dead. The sound that came out of her throat was halfway between a roar and a scream. '*Marina!*'

'Shhh –' I began, prodding her back.

Then the younger guard held up his lantern above me to light the small kitchen, and I saw what she'd been staring at.

My throat closed up. I couldn't speak.

Something must have alerted Marina and Horst to what was happening, to bring them running down to the kitchen in the middle of the night. They'd both changed out of their nightclothes, but for once, ever-proper Horst hadn't bothered with a jacket, which meant that he'd got dressed in a panicked hurry. Marina's black hair still hung down her back in a thick night-time plait ...

And they both lay crumpled on the tiled kitchen floor.

How long had they been lying there in the dark?

Horst's hand was stretched out towards Marina, but his gesture had fallen short, his dark brown fingers trailing agonising inches away from her shoulder.

Neither of them was moving.

Aventurine lunged forward, her human hands reaching out and her shadow exploding until it lashed a massive tail against the white walls in unison with her head-splitting roars of anguish.

Voices rose behind me, but I couldn't take in any of the words.

A candle lay flat on the floor next to Marina's outstretched fingers. Someone must have put it out after she dropped it, to stop any fires from racing through the room.

They'd *put out the candle*, but still left her lying helpless on the floor of the royal chocolate kitchen ...

Where I'd brought her.

'*Doomed to failure and pain and misery ...*'

Pain burst up jaggedly through my chest. I had to clap my hands over my mouth to stop myself from being sick.

Marina had never wanted to come to the palace in the first place. She hadn't understood why I would want to come either, leaving her beloved Chocolate Heart behind. But I'd been so certain I was gaining the chocolate house a glorious opportunity with this mission. I'd thought I was giving them a gift. I'd thought ...

'They're not dead.' Sofia's face was only inches away

from mine – when had she come so close? – and she shook my shoulders hard as she repeated herself. 'Silke, *they're not dead!* Can you even hear me?'

I twisted free with a jerk. Aventurine, Dieter and Jurgen were all gathered around those two prone bodies while the second guard stood at the doorway, keeping watch.

'They're not breathing,' Sofia said. 'But their hearts are still beating. They're just ... not moving. At all.'

'They've been enchanted into stillness.' Alfric looked across the kitchen with calm acceptance, as if nothing about the sight bothered him at all. 'It is Her Majesty's preferred method to subdue any groups she considers too harmless to require any more aggressive magics.'

'*Too harmless?*' Aventurine repeated. Against the wall, her shadowed wings rose around her, and her reptilian mouth opened wide. In her human face, before me, her golden eyes glowed with deadly fury. 'I'll show her *harmless!*'

'No.' I stepped forward, swallowing down the last of my bile. 'I will.'

I was the one who'd brought Marina and Horst there in the first place.

I was the one who'd flown away from my own parents tonight, after they'd given up everything for me and Dieter.

I didn't have claws or fire or food magic like Aventurine. I didn't have the fabulous riches or power of a princess. I would never gain the safe home at the palace that I'd dreamed of – I'd broken the palace walls instead – and I'd been sacked by the crown princess herself.

But I had true friends who cared about me, and more than that: I had myself.

If my time in this palace had taught me one thing, it was exactly who and what I truly was: not a spy after all, but a *storyteller*. That was something that no one could ever steal from me, no matter how powerful or magical they were.

'You make my chocolate', I told Aventurine. 'I'll handle the rest.'

I was ready to bargain with the fairies.

CHAPTER 26

Golden lights gathered around me with every step as I walked down a broad palace corridor not long afterwards, balancing a heavy tray in my hands. Fairy sentinels flew towards me from all directions, buzzing and swooping suspiciously around me in a cloud of dangerous, hot, sparkling light. All together, they let off a high-pitched collective hum that pierced my ears and sent pain shooting through my head with every step.

Alfric had kept the kitchen clear of them while I'd worked, but they rocketed wildly back and forth in front of me now, their sparks exploding in my eyes until I had to blink again and again to clear my vision. My fingers wanted to tremble, but I tightened my grip around the tray and didn't let myself flinch or slow.

I walked forward in my borrowed boots with my chin held high, not letting a single cup rattle in its saucer against the tray. Marina and Horst had opened their home and hearts to me. I wouldn't disrespect them with careless waitressing now. The tray in my hands was a silver statement of who and what I really was, and the fiery aftertaste of Aventurine's special hot chocolate filled my mouth like a reminder: I had been braving the world by myself since I was seven, but I didn't have to stand on my own any more.

When Alfric began to pull open the door to the grand gallery, another several lights shot through the widening crack towards me, joining the anxious cloud.

Just a few more steps ...

Two hot sparks touched the skin under my chin, and I almost jumped out of my boots.

They swept back into place on either side of my neck, just as they had earlier.

I knew these lights.

They pressed against my skin, humming with unmistakeable panic and doing everything they could to push me back out of danger.

When I was a little girl, I had always tried to do what my parents told me. Now I took a deep, steadying breath and held my ground instead. *I'm sorry*, I said silently to them both, *but you have to let me save you this time.*

Blinding white light spilled out to meet me as the door swung open. The golden lights in front of me scattered, clearing the way between me and their masters. Magic billowed through the air, tingling and terrifying.

I was in far over my head, and I knew it.

Ahead of me, the fairy king and queen sat, glowing and magnificent, on hulking, diamond-and-ruby-encrusted thrones in the centre of the long gallery. Those thrones hadn't just been placed on the gallery floor; they'd been *planted* there with massive, knotted tree branches that speared up through the tiled floor to anchor them in place. It was as if the earth itself had risen up to install their rule.

All around, bodies lay sprawled across the floor: armoured guards and battle mages, the strongest warriors in our kingdom. Every one of them lay as still as death, unbreathing.

Beyond them, the opposite doors stood cracked open, leading into the green darkness of another realm: *Elfenwald*.

Now our kingdoms really were connected.

Behind the thrones, the two fairy princes lounged against the tall, pitch-black gallery windows, looking as elegant and gorgeous as ever despite their yawns. A shifting crowd of colourfully robed fairy courtiers attended them as if this, tonight, were only another courtly function.

But not a single one of them could hold my attention once a flash of colour shifted in the corner of my vision. I wasn't the only human still awake in this room after all.

On my left, facing the two lavishly encrusted fairy thrones, sat my own crown princess, her dark eyes alert and watchful over the sparkling white web that tied her to a plain wooden chair. Her father lay slumped on the floor beside her, one big pink hand flung out against the tiles, but Princess Katrin watched everything with calm curiosity ... and when I caught her eye, she gave me a tiny, approving nod.

'*Silke*', the fairy queen said, and yanked back all of my attention. The force of my name in her bell-like voice rocked through my bones, until her shining, bitterly beautiful white face was all I could see. 'So', she purred, leaning back in her throne, 'you came crawling back after all. Did you ever really think you could escape us? Our sentinels are everywhere now. Soon the whole city will be under our control – and then the kingdom'.

'Is that what you imagine?' At the sound of Princess Katrin's voice, I jerked my gaze away from Queen Clothilde and found the crown princess watching us with her head tilted enquiringly. 'You may find it rather more difficult than you expect to control two kingdoms at once', she said. 'Our nation will react with outrage to this invasion'.

'Pah'. Queen Clothilde snorted. 'We dealt well enough with the rebellion in this palace, didn't we?' She pointed the tip of one polished red shoe at the black-robed man who lay closest to her. 'Those fools were the strongest battle mages you had. I hardly think your unwashed peasants will provide a greater challenge'.

'I beg your pardon?' I said. 'You're planning to send *everyone* to sleep if they argue with you? Across the entire *kingdom*?'

The crown princess gave a small, indulgent smile. 'Do let me know exactly how you plan to bring in the harvests with sleeping subjects, Your Majesty ... much less raise taxes, build new roads or –'

'Enough!' Queen Clothilde slammed one bejewelled hand down on the silver arm of her throne, her perfect face contorting with fury. 'We will do *whatever it takes* to preserve our safety, even if that means running this petty human kingdom into the ground!'

'But perhaps that won't be necessary.' Leaning back, King Casimir watched me through heavy-lidded eyes, his long, glowing brown fingers lying loosely along the arms of his own throne. 'I believe this girl is here to make us an offer. Aren't you, Silke?'

As I met his deep, sparkling gaze, I couldn't stop my throat from moving in a convulsive swallow. King Casimir's eyes always saw too much. As he looked at me now, I could swear he was inspecting me right down to the bone, peeling past all the layers of disguise that I had assumed over this past week.

I was just a girl from the riverbank. Who was I to even *try* to stand against him when all those adult battle mages and soldiers had already fallen in defeat?

I was *me*, that was who, and I was finished with trying to pretend to be anyone else from now on. So I lifted my chin and gave him my best storyteller's smile, clenching the muscles in my arms against the weight of the tray that I still held balanced in my hands.

'Your Majesty,' I said sweetly, 'isn't all this more trouble than it's worth? I know you've been hoping to destroy the dragons for good, but you've lost the only serious hostage you had. More than that, you've lost any chance of tricking the dragons into coming here on friendly terms and then ambushing them with whatever plan you'd cooked up.'

Queen Clothilde gave an impatient sniff. 'Do you think you know more about our plans than we do, little girl?'

'No,' I said, 'but I know more about dragons – because, unlike you, I want to *understand* them instead of killing them.' Ignoring the disdain on her face, I turned back to the fairy king. 'They would never have bothered to attack you before. Once they find out that you tried to abduct their hatchling, though, nothing will hold them back – certainly not *her* safety!' I tilted my head towards the tied-up crown princess. 'So you need to run now if you value your lives.'

'Nonsense.' The fairy queen's fingers tightened around the arm of her silver throne. 'Those beasts signed a treaty of mutual protection with Princess Katrin, and we're keeping her awake to remind them of that herself. They cannot risk harming her by attacking now.'

'You think not? Unlike you, dragons aren't magically compelled by their bargains.' I smiled slowly. 'You really hate that about them, don't you?'

'It hardly matters.' Queen Clothilde glared at me. 'Do you think us fools? Who else could have made the chocolate on your tray except that dragon-girl you've been trying to protect? She's clearly hiding somewhere here in this palace. Our sentinels will track her down within the hour, and –'

'Your *sentinels*?' I snorted. 'Your *prisoners*, you mean. What loyalty do you think any of them have to you? They hate you even more than I do!'

'You –!' She started up from her throne, already beginning to fling up one hand in preparation for attack.

I braced myself.

'Wait!' King Casimir gestured her back into her seat. 'What exactly are you saying, Silke? Why don't you take a moment to explain it all to both of us – and believe me ...' his deep, rich voice wrapped around me like invisible ropes holding me in place, 'it would be *most* unwise to lie to us now.'

Magic tingled with a sudden shock against my tongue. It felt thick and strange as I gulped, understanding that he would sense any lie that I tried to tell him from now on.

Luckily, a good storyteller knows how to use the truth.

'Let me tell you both a story,' I said with composure, and held out my tray. 'But first, would either of Your Majesties care for a hot chocolate to sweeten my tale? No?' I held the tray out a moment longer, expectantly, before I lowered it again, my muscles trembling with the strain. 'In that case ...'

I could feel Alfric's gaze on my back, waiting. It felt like support, even though he couldn't step in to help me if I failed.

Every story needs a good audience to succeed. And Alfric wasn't alone: all of the fairy courtiers I'd mingled with earlier were drawing closer to the thrones now, as if they couldn't resist the lure of a good tale either.

Alfric *had* told me that storytellers were a rarity underground.

I took a deep breath and smiled. 'Let me begin.'

'Once upon a time,' I said, 'there was a group of dragons who lived in the mountains near Drachenburg. They told stories to their hatchlings of the fairies who'd once caused them so much trouble, who would never stop their trickery or attacks, until the dragons finally gave in to necessity and ate the pests simply to be done with them.'

Outraged breaths hissed all around me, but I didn't let them slow me down. Horst and Marina were lying as still as death in the palace where I had brought them. I *would not* cosset their attackers' feelings now!

'Those fairies finally moved underground, much to the dragons' relief. They stayed there for over a century, until they'd been gone for so long that they became legendary mysteries to humankind, with nothing but stories and silver left to remember them by. Even among the dragons, the younger ones only really knew that fairies were tricksy and never to be trusted.

'What none of them realised was the more important truth: *fairies never trust.* That was why the fairies were so frightened of dragons in the first place: because full-grown dragons are immune to fairy magic. Those fairies couldn't bear for *anyone* to be their equals in power – much less their superiors. In fact, their own vulnerability frightened them so much that, after their last failed attack upon the dragons, they'd fled underground to escape even the possibility of any future defeats.

'Of course, they had to leave spies above ground to protect their kingdom. But they wouldn't risk the safety of any of their own kind – who were, after all, the only ones they cared about. Instead, they found another way.

'Some rulers might have made treaties or simple

agreements, respecting their partners and trusting their word. If they'd ever considered it ...' I had to clear my throat to keep emotion from thickening my voice. 'There are *so many* humans in the world who need real homes and help. There were even refugees from the wars up north who crossed their borders in search of safety, six years ago.' The lights against my neck pressed closer, and I had to restrain myself from tipping my chin to meet them.

'If those fairies had only offered them sanctuary in their green, forested kingdom above ground, they could have won themselves loyal friends and protectors for life. Those refugees would have been grateful to settle there forever as the fairies' eyes and ears above ground.

'But the fairies only trust creatures who have no choice but to obey them. So instead of inviting humans to live above ground as their friends, they captured human after human as their prisoners. They forced them, using threats and trickery, to accept poisoned bargains that turned them into magical golden lights, sentinels bound forever outside their own human bodies. Those fairies wouldn't accept anything but forced obedience *forever*.

'And they were so obsessed with protecting themselves from outside dangers that they didn't even realise what a dangerous mistake they were making ... or what a very large crack in their own armour they had created.'

'What crack?' Queen Clothilde demanded, leaning forward in her throne. 'What gibberish are you talking, girl?'

'You really can't see it?' I raised my eyebrows, scanning

the crowd of watching courtiers. Then I turned to the crown princess, still tied into her small, plain, wooden seat. 'You see it, don't you, Your Highness?'

'Oh, I see it.' Princess Katrin smiled with deep satisfaction, as the fairy queen glowered down at her and the fairy courtiers rustled with unease and interest.

I smiled at my ruthless ruler with, for once, perfect understanding. 'Of course you do,' I told her. 'You're famous for your diplomacy. In *your* political negotiations, everyone agrees to what you want, but you leave them thinking it was somehow what they wanted, too. You make every single group in the kingdom feel heard, so that everyone will think you're wonderful.'

'So?' The fairy queen shook her head impatiently. 'Weak human methods of gaining power don't concern us. We have magic beyond your mages' wildest dreams!'

'But diplomacy *isn't* weakness,' I said gently. 'It's strength. What do you think all of our *weak human* citizens will do when they hear you've taken over our kingdom and imprisoned our royals?'

King Casimir's fingers tapped lightly against his chair arm.

Queen Clothilde snapped, 'I told you already, they can't possibly stand against us.'

'But they'll try, because they're loyal and they actually *care*.' My hands were still occupied with the tray, but I tilted my head meaningfully towards the open door at the other end of the gallery, where green darkness led into another realm. 'Whereas in your kingdom ...'

Someone in the crowd sucked in a sharp breath.

'What *exactly* are you trying to say?' King Casimir enquired in a tone full of purring menace.

I looked up at him with wide, innocent eyes. 'Your Majesty', I said sincerely, 'I know it feels safer not to trust anyone else, so you never have to risk being betrayed ... or abandoned.' My voice shook, uncontrollably, on those last words. 'But humans – even humans without magic – aren't nearly as weak as you imagine. They think. They plot. They tell each other stories to build their courage when they're frightened. And because they're not all powerful, they work to *build alliances.*'

I let a smug smile spread across my face. 'Your sentinels are everywhere now, you've told us. That's not only true in our city, is it? You've spread them all across your own kingdom, too, to guard every secret entrance from invaders. That would be wise if they were your loyal spies and servants, but do you really believe that they're loyal to you? That they *want* to do any more than they absolutely have to?'

I stopped myself, with an effort, from glancing back at Alfric, who had taught me this final lesson just in time.

'You may have given your sentinels specific instructions when you left', I said, 'and in their current forms, I know they're magically bound to obey ... but every instruction has a loophole if you search hard enough. Especially if you're clever with language! So if someone *very* clever indeed – say, a storyteller who knows exactly how to twist her words – offers them dangerous new allies with fire and claws to win them freedom in a manner that doesn't break the *exact* orders they were given ...' My smile widened even more.

'*Enough!*' King Casimir's glowing fingers tightened into fists. 'No. More. Trickery!' Leaning forward, he pierced me with his glittering gaze. '*What bargain are you offering us, little girl?*'

I straightened my shoulders like a soldier making a report. 'I'm offering you the chance to free every one of your sentinels and all of the humans here, too, from their magical bindings – now and forever after.'

He gave a low, incredulous laugh. 'What great gift could you possibly offer us in return, to make such an extreme demand worthwhile?'

'Me?' I gave a casual shrug under the burning gaze of every single fairy in the gallery. 'Oh, I'm only a puny human with no magic, no fire, and no real teeth or claws of my own, so of course I couldn't offer you anything of value ... except ...' I smiled sweetly at him. 'I *could*, of course, tell the dragons *not* to invade Elfenwald with your own sentinels' help, using the brand new partnership I've just offered them. That *is* something I could do.

'So ...' I tilted my head and gave him my most inno-cent look. 'What do you say, Your Majesty? Tonight, do you accept *my* bargain?'

CHAPTER 27

The fairy courtiers erupted into confusion. Some ran towards the open doors, peering anxiously into the green darkness. Others rushed to protectively surround the thrones. Even the fairy princes lost their swagger, for once, and lunged across the gallery to take shelter behind their parents.

Golden lights swirled through the air like an agitated cloud of bees as King Casimir glared at me with wordless fury.

Queen Clothilde snapped, 'Don't be absurd! Why would the dragons band together with our sentinels? They're feral beasts, not treaty-builders!'

'They'd never allied with human kingdoms before either,' I said. 'Until now. Isn't chocolate wonderful?' Smiling, I lifted my tray higher.

'*Chocolate so sweet, it brokered a brilliant treaty.*' Laughter lurked in Alfric's voice.

'What?!' The fairy queen gasped, putting one hand to her glowing throat. 'You're a secret food mage! I should have known it. You *enchanted* that chocolate you gave the dragons. You slipped the magic through their mouths, just as we'd planned to do. You avoided their scales entirely!'

'Me? A food mage?' I widened my eyes. 'I've told you, I don't have any magic of my own.'

'Then what *is* in that chocolate?' The fairy queen inched back in her seat, her gaze fixed on my tray. 'And what would have happened to us if we'd drunk it?'

'Why don't you drink some now and find out?' I offered. 'After all, the dragons liked our hot chocolate when they drank it – less than an hour before they agreed to ally with us for the first time ever.'

Every word that I spoke was the absolute truth ... although *of course* none of the dragons' chocolate had been enchanted.

Aventurine would never use magic against her own family.

'They like my sister, too', Princess Katrin said smoothly. 'She's struck up quite a friendship with one of their hatchlings. So they should be more than happy to take her with them on their journey to Elfenwald ... where, I suspect, any sentinels you've imprisoned will be only too happy to accept her as our representative, offering them the safe refuge that they deserve.'

'Isn't it wonderful', I concluded happily, 'when so

many different kinds of people can come together instead of hiding away from one another?'

King Casimir leaped to his feet, his elegant cheekbones standing out in his suddenly gaunt-looking face. 'Do you have *any idea* how many of our people those dragons slaughtered in the past? My own father –'

'Was he attacking one of their nests at the time?' I held his furious dark gaze steadily. 'That's what happens when you attack someone just because you fear them. They fight back. And your sentinels have been waiting for their own chance to do that for a long time now. Whereas when people choose to work together and trust each other –'

'No more!' Clothilde was panting as she pointed at me. 'I will not be lectured by an impudent infant! You will stop talking and call back your horrible allies *now!*'

'Will I?' I raised my eyebrows at her with positively regal hauteur. 'Tonight I drank enchanted hot chocolate of my own, you know.' I lowered one eyelid in a wink ... and then I grinned my fiercest dragon-grin. 'What do you think it did to *me?*'

The fairy queen's glittering hairnet slipped as she whirled to stare wildly around the gallery ... and at the sparkling, golden lights that flew around it. Shuddering, she shrank back into her throne. 'Betrayal,' she whispered. 'Treachery!'

'I happen to know,' I told her softly, 'that Aventurine and Princess Sofia have already left. They're waiting on my signal now, but very soon, it'll be too late.'

Magic prickled in my mouth.

'She's telling the truth.' Rage vibrated in the fairy king's voice.

'Of course I am', I said serenely.

After all, Aventurine and Sofia *had* left the kitchen at exactly the same time that I had, although they'd taken a different direction. And although they were listening out for me to signal them, the spell in the hot chocolate that I'd drunk would only last for another fifteen minutes at the most. After that, I wouldn't be able to reach them.

So everything I'd said was exactly true ... but fairies weren't the only ones who could bend the truth for their own purposes.

'Don't you think it's time to give up now?' I asked gently. 'Why not let go of your old feud against the dragons? They've never attacked you except in self-defence.'

When the fairy queen looked back at me, I saw real anguish on her face. 'You don't understand,' she said, her voice raw. 'They could threaten my own *children* if they ever chose to come against us. My family's safety is at stake!'

I thought of my own parents, torn away from me and Dieter on her orders ... and of Marina and Horst lying helpless in the kitchen now. 'In that case, Your Majesty,' I said without a shred of sympathy, 'I would strongly suggest that you accept my bargain *right now*.'

Queen Clothilde took one look at the blackness beyond the tall glass windows. She took another look at the green darkness of the open door that led to her home. Finally, she met her husband's gaze.

'Oh, very *well*!' she snapped.

The fairy queen and king threw out their arms.

Lights flashed and flared all across the gallery, blinding me. I stumbled back. A cloud of thick green smoke billowed through the air. Coughing, I bent over my heavy tray. At the other end of the room, the great doors slammed shut with a bang that shook the walls of the palace.

The cloud of smoke cleared as suddenly as it had first appeared. Catching my breath, I slowly straightened, gripping the tray in my hands.

The fairies had gone. Alfric was gone. Even the massive thrones were gone, leaving broken floor tiles and tree roots behind them. The fairy web had gone, too, leaving the crown princess free, smoothing down her crumpled dressing gown and helping her father to his royal feet.

All around the gallery, guards, black-cloaked battle mages and dozens of new humans of all heights, skin colours and sizes were picking themselves up from the floor, coughing and staring around wildly in confusion.

And two more people were pushing themselves up from the floor on either side of me, where two golden lights had floated before.

My hands began to shake. Cups rattled in their saucers. The tray slipped and slid in my hands as I looked down at those two dark, familiar heads.

I couldn't even let myself breathe as they rose to their feet. If I did, the dream might break. Then I'd be back alone in my tent, with the wind whistling through its patchwork walls, and they'd be gone again.

I didn't dare let myself believe.

And then two tall, thin, weary-looking people were standing before me, tears streaming down their cheeks as they gazed at me with hungry eyes that I hadn't seen for far too long.

'Silke,' said my father for the first time in six years. His voice shook on the word. 'My little *Silke!*'

'*Oh!*' My mother threw her arms around me, sobbing openly.

I dropped my silver tray to the ground to hug her back. For once, I didn't even mind spilling hot chocolate or breaking a bit of crockery. As it all crashed to the ground, it made enough noise to wake a dragon, but it didn't break my beautiful dream ...

Because this was reality, and I'd won it. Every ounce of spilled chocolate was a worthy sacrifice.

Unlike the hot chocolate that I'd drunk earlier, this particular batch hadn't been enchanted anyway. It had only been for show, to aid my story – because every good storyteller knows just how useful visual props can be.

Dragons weren't the only ones who liked winning battles ... and fairies weren't the only ones who could be tricksy.

I'd forgotten what it felt like to be hugged as if you were the cherished centre of your mother's heart.

When my father wrapped his arms around the two of us in his own bear hug a moment later, I was surrounded by so much warmth that for the first time in a long time I felt utterly *safe*, from my head to my toes.

Then my mother let out a choked laugh, her tears sliding into my hair. Pulling back to look down at me, she said, 'Young lady, you put yourself into *so much danger*, I couldn't believe it. As soon as we finish here, you're going to be in *so much trouble!*' Her wide, generous mouth wobbled between a smile and another sob. 'I want to hear about *everything* that's happened to you – the *whole* story. Promise to tell me all of it as soon as you can?'

An irrepressible grin spread across my face, breaking through my own tears. I'd been waiting to share my stories with my mother for so long!

But I couldn't keep my parents to myself any longer. Someone else needed them, too.

So I finally used the spell that I had drunk with my own hot chocolate, so that I could – and *would* – call for their help if I really needed it. My friends had finally taught me that I didn't have to stand on my own after all.

'*Aventurine,*' I whispered. '*It's time.*'

A hidden door in the long gallery's wall swung open fifteen feet away.

Princess Sofia stepped through first, flanked by the two guards. As her gaze landed on her father and sister, her mouth dropped open. She grabbed the skirts of her dressing gown and started forward as if to run across the tiled floor to her family – but the crown princess gave her a look that stopped her in her tracks.

So Sofia walked the rest of the way with careful, princessy deportment, head held high and skirts rustling demurely. But the smile on her face lit the grumpy princess up like magic ... and the smile of unhidden pride that her older sister gave her then was one that I'd never seen from the crown princess before.

I didn't have time to watch the rest of their greetings. Aventurine stepped out next, her predatory golden gaze sweeping the room, probably hunting for any leftover fairy enemies. When her gaze landed on me, she gave me a fierce, approving grin and I grinned back at her.

See? I do have my own claws and fire after all!

Even the battle mages aimed looks of reluctant respect at the two of us as they brushed off their crumpled black robes. Once the people of Drachenburg found out that it was the threat of our dragon allies that had saved our kingdom from tonight's sinister fairy invasion ... well, attitudes towards my best friend and her family were going to be *very* different very soon.

I could have bounced with delight as I planned exactly how to write about it in my next brilliant, kingdom-crossing handbill ...

But the next person who stepped out of the hidden corridor was my older brother.

Ignoring all of my sensible arguments, Dieter had stubbornly insisted on waiting for me along with Aventurine and Sofia, just in case my plan failed and I needed help. I'd *told* him it was ridiculous to put himself in so much danger. There was no need to risk himself when he couldn't save me anyway ...

But the fact that he'd been so determined to try had

sent a hairline crack shooting through the defences that I'd been building against him for years. The expression on his face now, as he looked from me to our parents, made my whole chest feel like it was splitting wide open.

Standing in the palace gallery surrounded by strangers, my stiff and proud and angry older brother burst into helpless, wracking sobs. His shoulders shook as all the rigidity finally flooded out of him.

Our father reached him first. But I was the next to reach Dieter's side ... and for once, when I tentatively put my arms around him, he didn't even try to push me away.

It took a shockingly long time for me to realise that the crown princess was standing nearby waiting for me, with Princess Sofia at her side.

Royals were never meant to wait for anybody; it was the duty of their courtiers to wait on them. But it still took me a minute to untangle myself from the warm, solid huddle of my family, reunited at long last.

When I finally pulled free and dropped a curtsey, I could feel my mother's watchful, protective eyes on me. I did my best to curtsey gracefully, the way I'd learned over the past week, but my feet were swollen and burning in my borrowed boots, and the sleepless nights were catching up with me. I swayed on my feet as I straightened, and I gave Princess Katrin a giddy smile.

'Your Highness', I said, 'I trust I haven't disappointed you too much after all?'

The crown princess raised one elegant eyebrow. 'Well,'

she said, 'I can't imagine that we'll be signing any generous new trading agreements with Elfenwald ...' Her lips twitched. 'But you certainly did find out what they were after, as well as saving our kingdom. So, are you ready to take on your next assignment? I believe I could use your continued service in this palace after all.'

Sofia was smiling at me with rueful approval from her sister's side, all traces of hostility finally gone.

Aventurine watched us all with an expressionless face, but I knew she would support me, too. That was what dragons did when it came to family – and not only the family that you'd been born into.

I felt both of my parents' proud gazes resting on me as I looked back at the crown princess and felt all of my wildest dreams come true. After all, even now that we were back together, every member of my family would need to work hard to make a living. This shining offer was the most perfect ending to my mission that I could ever have imagined.

So I took a moment to savour the sheer wonder of being offered it in real life, with Dieter wide-eyed and watching beside me.

Then I curtseyed again, more deeply than ever. 'Your Highness', I said sincerely, 'I am deeply honoured by your offer. But I already have a home, and I value it far too much to give it up.'

The crown princess's second eyebrow shot up to match the first.

'A *home*?' Sofia repeated. 'But ...'

With a nod of my head, I turned away from the two princesses and all the luxury they were offering me.

'Come on,' I said to Aventurine, my brother and my parents. 'Let's find Horst and Marina.'

Home.

CHAPTER 28

Warm, rich, chocolate sweetness trailed up through the air as we led my parents down the servants' staircase. It tasted like home and it tasted like heaven ... and like everything I'd left behind so carelessly five days earlier.

My shoulders tightened at the memory. Why hadn't that part occurred to me before?

'I can't wait to introduce you to them,' I said to my parents. Sudden nerves crept into my voice, though, making it wobble.

What if Horst and Marina had already thought of another waitress to hire? One who didn't drag them into palaces and danger against their will?

They were fine now, I told myself. They *had* to be.

Everyone else had woken up unharmed from their enchanted sleep.

But if they blamed me for what they'd been through tonight, as they had every right to do …

When we neared the closed doorway, my parents both stopped.

'We'll wait here, actually, if you don't mind,' my mother told me. She drew Dieter down on to the step beside her, one arm cradled protectively around his lean shoulders. 'We need a few minutes alone with your brother.'

'Oh?' I stiffened, all of my instincts screaming alarm. I couldn't let a closed door stand between us. I never wanted to let them out of my sight again!

But as my father gave me a reassuring nod from Dieter's other side, I realised what they meant: they didn't want to make Dieter face anyone else right now. They were right.

My older brother's face was still ravaged with tears, and his eyes looked puffy behind his spectacles. He'd spent the last six years being strong for the sake of our family, no matter how much I resented the way that he had done it.

He was in no shape now to make small talk with near-strangers.

'I'm sorry,' he said in a tear-clogged voice. 'It's not that I don't respect your friends, Silke. Not really. It's just …'

'I understand.' I gave him a small, pained smile.

It was true. I really did, even though it might take years to heal all of the wounds that we'd dealt each other since our arrival in this city.

But nerves were boiling frantically underneath my skin now, worse with every passing moment, and the forced smile slipped away from my face as Aventurine pushed the door open.

Inside the small chocolate kitchen, a pot was boiling on the stove. Marina stood by the side counter, stirring something rich and brown in a mixing bowl. Her night-plaited black hair still hung down her back.

It all looked so homey. So perfect. So *comfortable*.

How could I have thrown it all away when the crown princess made me her first offer? And how could I convince them to take me back again now, after everything that had happened?

'There you are,' said Horst. He smiled at us both from the small wooden table near the stove. As he rose to his feet, I saw that he'd found a coat and a cravat since we'd last seen him. 'We've been waiting for you two.'

Aventurine, being Aventurine, didn't cry or hug either of them. She didn't even speak. But her fierce gaze devoured Horst and Marina as she stared them up and down, one at a time, visibly checking them both for injuries. Then she gave Horst a firm nod and joined Marina at the stove, shifting into place as seamlessly as silk.

Her place, as she'd realised from the first moment that she'd found them and stalked in to announce herself as their new apprentice.

Whereas I ...

I swallowed hard. 'How did you know that we would both be coming here?'

I'd closed the door behind me to give my family their privacy, but I couldn't seem to move any further into the room.

It had been all very well to grandly tell the crown princess that I already had a home when I was flush with confidence and success up there in the gallery. But now that I was here ...

I *knew* no one could take a safe home for granted. I'd spent the last six years learning that lesson; how could I have forgotten it even for a moment?

Horst frowned at me in what looked like confusion. 'Where else would the two of you come once it was all sorted out? We set off earlier to hunt you down when things first went wrong, but when we woke up and realised *someone* must have broken the spell ...'

'Well, who else could it have been? You think the royals or their fancy-cloaked mages could have managed it? Pah.' Marina finally turned around to look at me. 'At least you haven't got yourself hurt this time. *That's* a mercy.' She shook her head as she turned back to the stove. 'But if there ever was a girl who could learn to *stand still* from time to time ...'

'I think – I might be ready to try.' Taking a deep breath, I looked at her strong, solid back and felt my mind go utterly blank. Where had all of my clever words gone? I'd been telling stories all night to fairies and goblins and royals, but now that I was back with the people whose opinions really mattered, my tongue and my head both felt thick and clumsy. 'I mean, I thought I might ... if you don't mind ...'

'She turned down the crown princess's job offer,' Aventurine said flatly. Then she rolled her eyes at me over her shoulder. 'That *is* what you're trying to spit out, isn't it?'

'You did *what*?' Blinking, Horst sank back down into his seat. 'But, Silke, I thought you wanted –'

'I ...' I closed my eyes, so I wouldn't have to see their faces. My words came out in a mangled, graceless rush: 'I-told-them-I-already-had-a-home!'

My whole body strained backwards towards the doorway as I spoke, preparing to spin away as quickly as possible the moment that yet another piece of solid ground went sliding out from under my feet.

It would be all right. I knew how to start over. I –

Marina's snort was so loud, it made my eyes fly open. 'It took you long enough to realise it! Good lord.' She turned to Horst. 'Best waitress in the city, clever like you wouldn't believe *and* there isn't a customer alive who can resist her stories about our chocolate. How long have we been trying to pin her down now? Months!'

'You ... have?' Shaking my head, I looked at Horst for confirmation.

His smile warmed me like the best hot chocolate. 'Well, of course we have,' he said gently. 'Why do you think we didn't hire another waitress when you left? Or hire a second waitress in the first place, when you would only agree to work part-time?'

'But ...' I looked back at Marina. 'I know you didn't want to come to the palace for this visit. If it hadn't been for me –'

'If it hadn't been for you, we would have closed down months ago, as you're the only one in this shop with a real head for business.' She narrowed her eyes at me. 'Did you think we hadn't noticed that? Or that we couldn't have wriggled out of this palace invitation if we'd wanted to?' Marina shrugged. 'We weren't about to let you march into danger without us. Once we'd found you, girl, why on earth would we ever want to let you go?'

My throat thickened. I couldn't hold her gaze. As my eyes misted, I ducked my head down quickly. My gaze landed on the table ...

... Where I saw that Horst had set out four places, not just three, for tonight.

It was true that the walls of the Chocolate Heart might one day close, if the business went under. Unlike the palace, that small shop hadn't been designed to last for centuries – and even the mighty palace walls had broken tonight. No building could last forever. But the home that Marina and Horst had offered me ever since we'd first met – that warm, safe spot where I never had to be anyone but myself to win their approval ...

That could never be taken from me after all. And it was worth so much more than any royal court.

'Here.' Marina filled one of the delicate porcelain cups and held it out to me. 'You'd better be the one who tries this new blend first. Tell me what you think.'

'Me?' I let out a half-laugh of disbelief as I accepted the steaming cup and sat down at the table. The new blend of hot chocolate smelt incredible, of course, but I hesitated with my arm still held out towards Marina. 'I'm not the chocolate expert here, you know.'

'Don't worry', Aventurine said from the stove. 'I can already tell you what to say just from smelling it: there isn't enough chilli in this one.'

'Not enough for *you*, dragon-girl!' Marina gave her a light tap on her shoulder, lips twitching indulgently. 'But I designed *this* particular blend for someone who doesn't breathe fire. She deserves her own drink, too, don't you think?'

The thin gold-and-white cup warmed my hands through its silver casing. My head whirled. The smell of chocolate filled my senses. I closed my eyes, took a breath and lifted the cup to take a long, deep sip.

Ravishing sweetness filled my mouth, replete with flavours I didn't know how to name. It tasted like warm spices and adventures, winter and hope – and *love*, a rich chocolate centre to it all.

For once, I couldn't speak. I felt too full – full of gratitude, full of happiness, full of *everything*.

'Well?' Horst said. 'It's yours, you know. Marina's been fiddling with it for weeks, trying to get it just right, but I liked it from the beginning. What do you think? Shall we put it on the menu when we get back home?'

I had cried enough tonight to flood a barge. So I told myself, with all my might, that I *wouldn't* cry again. But as I opened my eyes, I found that I didn't want to.

As spicy-sweet chocolate filled my belly with warmth, I felt a brand new story spinning out from beneath my feet, carrying me in directions I had never let myself dream about before. Now that I'd finally found my own home and safety ...

If my handbills could be read and passed around the continent, why shouldn't I use them to help everyone I cared about – the dragons, my family and friends on the riverbank, *and* my Chocolate Heart family, too?

I would tell my own story with all of my heart, until everyone in my city felt it in their hearts, too ... and then, together, we would remake the world.

'I love it,' I said. 'And I am going to write the *best* handbills about it. Just you wait and see what I can do!'

ACKNOWLEDGEMENTS

This is a book that requires a lot of heartfelt thanks to all of the people who made it possible. First and foremost, I am so grateful to my editor, Ellen Holgate, for her smart, compassionate and incisive edits, which made this story so much stronger. I may have occasionally cried and cursed as I struggled through my rewrites, but I am sincerely glad now to have done them. Thank you for holding me to high standards and having steadfast faith that I could achieve them!

As always, my husband, Patrick Samphire, gave me endless support along the way, patiently rereading draft after draft, keeping me well stocked in my favourite chocolate, and talking me through every single crisis in confidence. Patrick, I will never be able to bake you enough chocolate-chip cookies to properly express my gratitude! But I will keep on making them anyway (and only stealing some of them).

Claire and Philip Fayers gave me a retreat exactly when I most needed it, letting me hole up in their lovely home for several days, lending me soft, sweet cats to pet, and feeding me delicious meals and gourmet tea to fuel me through my rewrites. Later, my parents, Richard and Kathy Burgis, did heroic amounts of babysitting to give me time to work, and my brother David Burgis was a wonderful sounding board as I worked out plot issues. I appreciate all of you so much!

Thank you to the brave friends who beta-read first-draft chapters of the book and cheered me on as I wrote them: Jenn Reese, R.J. Anderson, Deva Fagan, Rene Sears, Beth Bernobich, Tricia Sullivan, Patrick Samphire and Tiffany Trent. And thank you to the friends who critiqued part or all of this novel at any stage: Tiffany Trent, Jenn Reese, Patrick Samphire, Tina Connolly, Deva Fagan, Rene Sears, R.J. Anderson, Aliette de Bodard, Anne Nesbet and Jaime Lee Moyer.

Thank you to my wonderful agent, Molly Ker Hawn, for reassuring me just when I needed it most, and for being the best possible partner in my publishing career. I feel so lucky to be your client! And thank you to Sarah Shumway for finding just the right title for the book when I was at the point of total despair about it.

Thank you to Emma Bradshaw, Grace Whooley, Charlotte Armstrong and Lizz Skelly for all of the amazing marketing and publicity support that you've given to both of my books with Bloomsbury. I appreciate you guys so much!

Thank you to Lucy Mackay-Sim for the thoughtful line edits, which made such a difference. Thanks to Helen Vick for beautifully managing the final editorial stages, thank you to Madeleine Stevens for the wonderful copy-edits, and thank you to Fliss Stevens for carefully overseeing the final proof stages. This book is about finding a real community, and I've been so happy to be a part of the lovely Bloomsbury community!

And most of all, thank you to my wonderful sons, who have brought me back to storytelling out loud, who tell me fabulous stories of their own, and who inspire me every single day.

FIND OUT HOW AVENTURINE
CAME TO DRACHENBURG IN

The Dragon with a Chocolate Heart

AVAILABLE NOW

READ ON FOR A SNEAK PEEK ...

CHAPTER 1

I can't say I ever wondered what it felt like to be human. But then, my grandfather Grenat always said, 'It's *safer not to talk to your food*,' – and as every dragon knows, humans are the most dangerous kind of meal there is.

Of course, as a young dragon, all I ever saw of them were their jewels and their books. The jewels were delightful, but their books were just maddening. What a waste of ink! No matter how hard I squinted, I could never make it past the first few paragraphs of cramped, crabby text. The last time I tried, I got so frustrated I burned three of those books to cinders with angry puffs of my breath.

'Don't you have any higher feelings?' my brother demanded, when he saw what I'd done. Jasper wanted to be a philosopher, so he always tried to stay calm, but his tail began to lash dangerously, sending gold coins showering through our cavern as he glared at the smoking pile before me. 'Just think,' he told me. 'Every one of those books was written by a creature whose brain was half the size of one of your forefeet. And yet, apparently, even *they* have more patience than you!'

'Oh, really?' I loved goading high-minded Jasper into losing his temper ... and now that I'd laid waste to my tiny paper enemies, I was ready for fun. So I braced myself, scales rippling with secret delight, and said, 'Well, I think anyone who wants to spend his time reading ant scribbles must have an ant-sized brain himself.'

'Arrrrgh!'

He let out the most satisfying roar of rage and leaped forward, landing exactly where I'd been sitting only a moment ago. If I hadn't been expecting it, I would have been slammed into a mountain of loose diamonds and emeralds, and my still-soft scales would have been bruised all over. But Jasper was the one who landed there instead, while I joyously pounced on his back and rubbed his snout in the pile of rocks.

'Children!' Our mother raised her head from her fore-feet and let out a long-suffering snort that blew through the cave, sending more gold coins flying. 'Some of us are trying to sleep after a long, hard hunt!'

'I would have helped you hunt,' I said, jumping off Jasper. 'If you'd let me come –'

'Your scales haven't hardened enough to withstand even a wolf's bite.' Mother's great head sank back down towards her glittering blue-and-gold feet. 'Let alone a bullet or a mage's spell,' she added wearily. 'In another thirty years, perhaps, when you're nearly grown and ready to fly ...'

'I can't wait another thirty *years!*' I bellowed. My voice echoed around the cave, until Grandfather and both of my aunts were calling their own sleepy protests down the long tunnels of our home, but I ignored them. 'I can't live cooped up in this mountain forever, going nowhere, doing nothing –'

'*Jasper* is using his quiet years to teach himself philosophy.' Mother's voice no longer sounded weary; it grew cold and hard, like a diamond, as her neck stretched higher and higher above me, her giant golden eyes narrowing into dangerous slits focused solely on me, her disobedient daughter. 'Other dragons have found their own passions in literature, history or mathematics. Tell me, Aventurine: have you managed to find *your* passion yet?'

I ground my teeth together and scratched my front right claws through the piled gold beneath my feet. 'Lessons are boring. I want to explore and –'

'And how, exactly, do you plan to communicate with the creatures you meet on your explorations?' Mother asked sweetly. 'Or have you been progressing further with your language studies than I had imagined?'

Jasper let out a muffled snicker behind me. I swung around and shot a ball of smoke at him. He let it explode harmlessly in his face, his eyes gleaming with amusement.

'I can speak six languages already,' I muttered as I turned back to Mother.

Still, I couldn't quite lift my head to meet her gaze.

'By the time she was your age,' Mother said, 'your sister could speak and write twenty.'

'Hmmph.'

I didn't dare snort smoke at Mother. But I would have snorted it at Citrine if she had been stuck here with us, instead of living far away in her perfectly extraordinary, one-of-a-kind, dragon-sized palace. Citrine wrote epic poetry that filled other dragons with awe and was worshipped like a queen by every creature who came near her.

No one could measure up to my older sister. There was no point even trying.

I could feel Mother's gaze on me grow even sharper, as if she'd read my thoughts. 'Language,' she said, quoting one of Jasper's favourite philosophers, 'is a dragon's greatest power, reaching far beyond the realm of tooth and claw.'

'I know,' I muttered.

'Do you really, Aventurine?' Her long neck curved as her massive head swung down to look me in the eyes. 'Because courage is one thing, but recklessness is quite another. You may think yourself a ferocious beast, but outside this mountain you wouldn't survive a day. So you had better start being grateful that you have older and wiser relatives to look after you.'

Mother was sleeping deeply only two minutes later, her heavy breaths *whoosh*ing as calmly and evenly through the cavern as if we'd never even had an argument.

'Not a day?' Jasper whispered, once she was safely asleep. He shook off the last of the gemstones clinging to his back, and grinned at me, showing all of his teeth. 'Not an hour, more likely. Not even half an hour, knowing you.'

I glared at him, mantling my wings. 'I could look after myself perfectly well. I'm bigger and fiercer than anything else in these mountains.'

'But are you smarter?' He snorted. 'I'd wager all the gold in this cavern that even wolves are better at philosophical debates than you. And they probably don't set things on fire every time they lose!'

'Ohhh!' I whirled around, lashing my tail. But there was no escape. The cavern walls were too close, and feeling closer with every second. They were pushing in around me until I could barely breathe.

And I was supposed to spend another thirty years trapped inside this mountain, listening to my relatives tell me off for the fact that it was boring?

Never.

That was when I realised exactly what I had to do.

But I wasn't stupid, no matter what anyone thought. So I waited until Jasper finally gave up teasing me and curled up with one of his new human books – one that I hadn't burned. It was a philosophical tract, so I knew I would be safe.

'I'm going on a walk through the tunnels,' I told him, when he had flicked the pages five times with his claw.

'Mm-hmm,' Jasper murmured, without looking up. 'Aventurine, listen to this: this fellow thinks it's morally wrong to eat meat. And fish, too! He won't hurt any breathing creatures, so he only eats plants. Isn't that fascinating?'

'*Fascinating*? He's going to starve!' I flicked my ears in horror. 'I told you humans had pebbles for brains!'

But my brother didn't even hear me. Smoke trickled in a long, happy stream through his nostrils as he held the tiny book close to his eyes, rumbling with satisfaction.

I stepped right over his tail, one foot after another, on my way to freedom.

Rattling snores echoed down the long tunnels from the caverns where Grandfather Grenat, Aunt Tourmaline and Aunt Émeraude slept. Luckily, at this time of day, when the sun was at its highest, no one was likely to wake at a few scrabbling sounds from the corners of the mountain. Dropping to my belly, I wriggled my way up the side tunnel I'd discovered two years earlier, the one that was too small for any of the grown-ups to use. At the very top, filled and hidden by a boulder the size of my head, was a secret entrance to the mountain. It was my favourite spot in the world.

I'd shown Jasper of course, ages ago, but he almost never visited it – only when I dragged him there. He was always happiest curled up in our cavern with a book, or scratching out long, wordy treatises with one foreclaw dipped in ink.

I was the one who loved pushing the boulder free and poking the tip of my snout out of the hole, to take deep, tingling breaths of the fresh, outside air and watch the clouds float through the sky overhead. I'd never dared to go any further, but I lay there for hours sometimes, just dreaming of the day when I would finally be allowed to stretch my wings and fly across the endless sky.

Today, for the first time ever, I wasn't going to stop at dreaming.

I was going to show Jasper – *and* Mother – just how capable I was of taking care of myself. Then the grown-ups would have no excuse to keep me hidden away any longer.

With exhilaration flooding through me, I folded my wings tightly against my sides and lunged for the outside world and freedom.

It was harder than I'd expected to squeeze out of the hole. My shoulders stuck in the opening until I nearly roared with effort. I had to bite my mouth shut and swallow down choking smoke to keep myself silent. Finally, *finally*, I forced myself free with an explosive *pop!* It sent me tumbling on to the ground outside ... and whimpering with pain. My folded wings had scraped so hard against the rough, craggy edges of the rocks that there were ragged tears, now, in my silver and crimson scales.

What had Mother said? *'Your scales haven't hardened enough to withstand even a wolf's bite ...'*

I gnashed my teeth and pushed myself up on to all four feet, babying my wings by holding them half folded at my side. Every breeze that blew across them made me wince, but I growled away the pain.

So, I wouldn't be making my first attempt at flight today. Never mind. I didn't need to fly to catch my prey.

For the first time in my life, the sky arched blue and free all around me, and I was free, too. The jagged peak of the mountain rose behind me. Below me lay a forested valley. And in between, buried somewhere in the rumpled foothills and narrow, rocky paths where animals and humans made their tiny ways ...

I set off down the mountainside, following the scent of food.